"I Never Force, Annie."

His hand slipped down her cheek and found the pulse in her neck, pounding slowly against the slight pressure of his massaging thumb. "I only have to ask," he said softly.

Her eyes had fluttered shut. They snapped open. "Now you're being purposely obnoxious. Besides, this won't help you. It will interfere with what I'm trying to teach you."

"Teach me." He touched her waist, making her insides feel as quivery and airy as soap bubbles. "Teach me, Annie," he repeated more strongly, an air of desperation in his words.

"Cliff, you can have everything you had before, believe me. The accident hasn't made you any less attractive."

"Then come here."

His hand closing on the bare skin of her arm was like the first blast of shower spray in the morning. She had to brace herself for it.

He felt her stiffness. "I can have women, I just can't have you, is that it?"

Dear Reader:

What makes a romance? A special man, of course, and Silhouette Desire is celebrating that fact with twelve of them! From June 1989 to May 1990 every month will spotlight an irresistible Silhouette Desire hero — our *Man of the Month*.

February's *Man of the Month* comes from the pen of Dixie Browning. Clement Cornelius Barto is a unique hero who is sure to charm you with his unusual ways. But make no mistake, it's not just *Beginner's Luck* that makes him such a winner.

March brings you a man who's double the fun, because not only is Jody Branigan an exciting hero, he's also one of Leslie Davis Guccione's Branigan brothers. Look for his story in *Branigan's Touch*.

Don't miss these men!

Please write to us:

Jane Nicholls
Silhouette Books
PO Box 236
Thornton Road
Croydon
Surrey
CR9 3RU

TERRY LAWRENCE

BEFORE DAWN

Silhouette Desire

Originally Published by Silhouette Books
a division of
Harlequin Enterprises Ltd.

First published in Great Britain in 1990
by Silhouette Books, Eton House, 18-24 Paradise Road,
Richmond, Surrey TW9 1SR

© Mary Terese Lawrence 1989

Silhouette, Silhouette Desire and Colophon are
Trade Marks of Harlequin Enterprises B.V.

ISBN 0 373 57832 6

22 – 9003

Made and printed in Great Britain

TERRY LAWRENCE

told her fifth-grade teacher she wanted to be a writer. He sent her home with a note to her mother saying, "I believe Terry possesses a gift and should be encouraged." In the twenty years that followed, that encouragement has come from family, friends and other teachers, all of whom made it easier for her to achieve her dream.

She lives in northern Michigan, where she divides her time and attention between a word processor, a cat and four breathtaking seasons.

Another Silhouette Book by Terry Lawrence

Silhouette Desire

Cabin Fever

One

Annie Rosetti had few rules she lived by. Accept your-self for what you are. Be honest. Don't get too hung up on what others think. And *never* get involved with a heartstoppingly handsome man. Watching Cliff Sulli-van stride down the beach, she had a sinking feeling he'd be the exception to the rule.

It was that period in mid-August when even the breeze off the big lake couldn't cool things down. Maybe that justified his wearing nothing but threadbare cutoffs and weathered Topsiders. Annie could almost feel the ra-diating heat of the sun on his bare chest. She squeezed her eyes shut, shook her head and patted the black dog beside her.

Okay, so Cliff Sullivan was Blond, Bearded, Brawny and Beautiful. Annie tried to think of another word that began with a *B* and spelled trouble. Bothersome was as close as she got.

Oh, yes—and Blind.

Cliff stopped fifty feet away, planted strong hands on narrow hips and shouted for his dog. "Kane! Damn you, get back here!"

He reminded her of the blinded Samson, tearing down the temple in a rage. But she seriously doubted that Samson wore black wraparound shades, and every fiber in her body insisted that Samson had never been that good-looking.

"Kane!"

The black Lab whose leash Annie held barked and lunged, almost yanking her arm out of its socket.

"Over here!" she called out.

She watched Cliff half turn in their direction. Anyone else would think the man wore dark glasses because they made him look so damn good. She would have. And she would have steered clear. Even now a tiny voice inside her was shouting a warning. This was not a man to get mixed up with. But—

He needs me and he doesn't even know it.

Damn.

Cliff strode in the direction of his barking dog. Watching the anger and strength he put into something as basic as walking, it was obvious to Annie that he was a man who did nothing halfway. He'd been avoiding her art therapy classes at the hospital just as bullheadedly. But she and Cliff Sullivan were about to collide.

As she watched him walk toward her, she scanned the sand for anything that might get in his way. He wasn't using a cane. From what she'd heard, he wouldn't. For someone who'd been blinded only three weeks before in a blasting accident, he didn't hesitate.

He's either very confident or completely denying his limitations, Annie thought. Meanwhile the dog at her side was barking his fool head off.

"Kane!"

"I've got him."

"Quiet!"

Not easily affronted, Annie couldn't prevent a startled "What?" from escaping her.

"I was talking to the dog," he spat.

Annie took a deep breath and decided she might as well be direct. "You've been avoiding me."

He stopped within ten feet of her. His hair was sun-bleached with darker strands underneath; his beard was long stubble. Neither the heavy stubble nor the sunglasses could hide the emotions flickering across his face: confusion, frustration, anger.

"Say that again," he demanded.

He was reaching, getting her to talk so he would know which direction to turn, Annie figured. "If you want to know where I am, you're right on target."

He stiffened.

Annie counted to ten while waiting for him to speak, the sound of the waves and sea gulls punctuating the silence.

Finally Cliff stuck his hand out, seemingly deciding to ignore the whole blindness issue. "May I have the leash?"

"You're not going to hit him, are you?"

He appeared surprised for a moment, until the anger reemerged. This time it was directed at himself. "How can I hit him if I can't even find him? Please?" He ground the word out between his teeth.

Annie placed the leash in his hand, Kane's cue to leap on his chest. "Down, damn it!"

Despite the show of anger, Annie glimpsed the way his hand lingered momentarily on the back of the dog's neck, giving it an unobtrusive squeeze. When he shoved the dog down, the robust Lab interpreted it as play and immediately assumed the position—paws down, rear end in the air, his whole body swaying with each energetic wag of his tail.

Annie had to laugh. There was something about the way a dog rebounded from rejection and temporary setbacks. Unlike some people. She studied Cliff a moment. "How old is he, your dog?"

"Eight months of trouble."

"A little young to be a seeing-eye dog, isn't he?"

"You mean a little untrained?"

"Uh-huh."

Cliff paused. He was beginning to pick up on so many subtle clues about this unseen woman. He could hear her smiling, and that surprised him. He'd figured that by this time he'd be contending with pity. "He's not really a seeing-eye dog."

"And you're not really blind?"

Cliff straightened at that one, pulling his shoulders back, the muscles on his chest taut. No, he wasn't blind. At least, he wouldn't be after the operation. "It's temporary. Is it that obvious?"

"Kane was dragging this harness through my tomato plants, the kind guide dogs use." He flinched as she unexpectedly put the harness in his hand, then flushed at his own response. His fist tightened around the square leather bar.

Knowing apologizing would only make it worse, Annie took a moment to chalk up a few more impressions. He hated talking about it. And, God, how he hated being helped.

She took a chance and laughingly asked, "So where'd you get those crazy shades?" One of them had to relax; if he didn't, he'd crack.

"I like 'em dark," was all he said.

Her voice came out huskier than the crashing of the waves. "And I like 'em blond," she said, almost to herself.

Cliff smiled automatically, thrown off balance by the sound of flirtation in her voice. Maybe he was imagining it. After all, how could he tell if he couldn't see? "That's a problem?"

On him even half a smile was gorgeous. Annie's heart skittered like a sandpiper chased up the sand. "It is when they don't like me."

He mulled that over a moment. "They must be blind."

Annie's smile widened, and she chuckled so he could hear it. That might have been the first joke he'd made about his sight since the accident. She was careful not to pat herself on the back for making progress so soon; they still had a long way to go. If only she could get him into her class...

"I work with the blind, you know. My name's Annie Rosetti."

Her progress ended quickly as he muttered an ugly curse. "The hospital sent you."

She crossed her arms. "Sorry I didn't get around to that sooner. You *have* been avoiding me, Mr. Sullivan."

If he could see, he'd be looking down at her. "I don't need to make baskets," he sneered.

"Pottery. And I believe we have a date for two o'clock tomorrow. You've already broken four of them."

"I won't be seeing you." A miserable play on words. Cliff clenched his jaw when he realized it. A wave of fury washed over him. She'd known who she was talking to all along. He hadn't. It was an underhanded trick, and she had the gall to laugh. His gut tightened at the sound and his mouth compressed in a thin line.

"Maybe you won't be seeing me, Cliff, but I promise I'll be seeing you."

She looked him up and down once more. Virile, vital and ready to lash out at something, anything. Trouble is, fate was hard to hit. "You've got a lot of anger built up in you—"

"So you're a psychologist-potter, is that it? Have clay, will diagnose?"

Cliff damned himself for making her laugh again. Encased in a world of milky white light, her laughter was the last thing he wanted. There was an earthiness there that struck a chord in him. He didn't like coy women, and this one sounded uninhibited, sexy and much too pleased with everything he said.

"Caught me analyzing without a license. Honestly, Cliff—"

Did she always pause after his name, or did he imagine that, too?

"—stop by my class. You might learn something—like how to deal with your handicap. I mean, training a pet to be a seeing-eye dog is one way—"

"I'm blind, damn it. Not handicapped, not disabled. I hate those bloody euphemisms. And for your information, I don't need to learn to live with anything, because this condition's temporary."

"Probably." If he expected an argument, she wasn't going to give it to him. From what she'd gathered at the hospital, the kind of corneal scarring he had could often be cured with a transplant. They did them every day downstate. But the waiting list could take months, and the procedure wasn't guaranteed. "So what are you going to do temporarily until this little setback clears up?"

"I'll get by."

They were butting heads, getting nowhere. Difficult as it was, Annie let the silence stretch, let him turn and walk away, Kane leading like a sturdy black tugboat.

Ten feet farther down the beach, Cliff stopped. Why, he couldn't have said. It wasn't polite to just turn his back on her. Then again, he hadn't been feeling very polite for the past three weeks. Caged, was more like it.

He faced her, he hoped, and nodded toward the straining dog. "He's been in a kennel for a month. They exercise them, but he really needs to run."

So do you, Annie thought. Body honed as only a runner's could be, he'd probably worked out every day before the accident. No wonder he was a seething mass of energy.

But more importantly, he was talking. Innate politeness, loneliness—she'd never know. Either way it was an opening. Annie did everything but jump at it. She sauntered up beside them instead.

"I'm not up for a run, but how about a good long walk?" Not waiting for an invitation, her footfalls hissed softly ahead of them in the sand. Man and dog had no choice but to follow.

He'd been rude, Cliff knew. He'd been biting off everybody's head lately. Just because he had a better than average excuse...

He'd also been a real jerk about those therapy classes they'd tried to get him into at the hospital. Hell, as long as he had his brother staying with him at the beach house, what did he need with therapy? Playing with clay wasn't going to teach him a damn thing about how to get through this nightmare, sane.

Eventually his thoughts strayed to the woman walking beside him. She'd tricked him, tracking him down on the beach without introducing herself. He tried to get worked up about that again, but he couldn't. Somehow it was a relief just having someone there. He tried to picture her. There was something about her voice. It was smooth, one or two notes lower than typical. A woman's voice, not a girl's. She could be anywhere up to forty and matronly as a TV nurse.

They walked in silence. Cliff waited for the inevitable question about the explosion that had blinded him. She didn't ask.

"Ow!"

"Halt." He jerked the dog to a stop when the word itself didn't work. "What is it?"

Annie put her hand on his arm to steady herself as she pulled off one of her rubber thongs. "Little stones in the sand. One got into my sandal."

Her hand was small, cool on his skin. "Flip-flop," he corrected automatically.

They both stood amazed for a moment.

"Very good," she murmured.

Even Cliff was impressed. Every day he was able to put more together by using his other senses. Not that it helped anywhere near enough. For example, it didn't tell him anything about what she looked like. That his curiosity couldn't be satisfied only added to his frustration. At this point in his life, he had no business being curious about any woman.

"Your hearing is very acute," Annie commented.

"Sounds like another diagnosis," he replied curtly.

"Oh-oh. Better report me to the AMA."

Although her barefoot steps were softer without the slap of thongs, Cliff could just as easily follow the gentle sounds. He imagined her feet, and from there, since he couldn't picture her face, he contented himself with trying to picture her legs.

"Blond or brunette?" The question popped out. He was startled he'd even spoken.

Annie smiled, careful to keep it out of her voice. "Who, me?"

She noticed he was seething again. Oh, he hated asking for anything, didn't he? But she couldn't help feeling good. He was reaching out, seeking some form of contact.

"Yeah, you," he growled. "I know what Kane looks like."

Her smile widened. She'd reward him for that. "Medium brown hair, brushing my shoulders. Remarkable only for its total frizziness. I hold it back with combs most of the time."

"About five foot five, right?"

She whistled, one clean musical note that showed she knew how.

Cliff smiled. Nailed it, as his brother Dave would say. He was getting good at this.

"How did you figure that one out?" she asked.

"The length of your stride, how much shorter it is than mine. Sometimes it helps to have an engineering background."

"This is soft sand," she argued. "It's clumsy to walk on and you're on the hardpack by the water."

"Therefore?"

"Therefore, my steps are shorter because the terrain is more difficult, and *that* was an educated guess."

He grinned. "Darn right."

"Do you guess weights, too?"

"You wouldn't like it if I was right."

"Give it a shot."

"One-twenty?"

"You're right. I don't like it," she admitted, laughing. At least he was taking some pride in the sharpening of his other senses. That would help them both.

He couldn't resist one more. "You're not wearing a bathing suit, even though you're on the beach."

Now she *was* impressed. The fact was that she had nothing on under her sundress except some silk panties. "Superman, right? You wear those shades to hide your X-ray vision."

"I can hear the fabric flapping. It has to be a dress. Simple."

"Ah." It was an Indian cotton, a complicated blue vine printed on a gray background, imported by an artist friend of hers. Tentlike and comfortable, flimsy and cool, she liked to toss it on for beach walks. With the breeze picking up, the dress flapped around and between her legs with every step. "Of course, I could be wearing a bathing suit under it."

"Could be."

"Anything else, Amazing Kreskin?"

"You're carrying those flip-flops in your left hand. I can feel the sand sprinkle my leg when you swing them."

"Oh, sorry." Yes, she was. Especially after she glanced down at those legs. Golden and hairy and built like the towers Samson toppled. Muscles rippled with every step. No wonder he wanted to run. She felt like running herself. In the opposite direction.

"Anything else you want described?" he asked.

"I'm not wearing anything else—" Blood rushed to her cheeks. She knew if she stopped to stare at that grin on his face, they'd be here for hours. Fortunately the dog intervened by lurching to the right and panting excitedly. "Looks like Kane wants to head up there," she said, pointing in the direction the dog was lunging.

Cliff's mood abruptly changed. He had to pay more attention to his surroundings. No more walking on the beach, drifting, thinking, working out problems. Just getting to and from home was a problem now.

"He's probably heading for the cottage," he said.

"Cottage! Looks more like House Beautiful. Peaked roof, lots of glass, bleached siding and matching snow fence?"

He silently thanked her for the clues. It was his place. "Keeps sand from drifting against the house."

Kane barked his barrel-chested bark until they reached the gate. There was an uncomfortable pause while Cliff wound the leash around his fist. He'd have to thank her for getting him here. He used to be polite; lately he was beginning to hate every thank-you. Each one seemed like another bar on his cage.

"Excuse me if I'm bad at this. I haven't always depended on the kindness of strangers."

Annie smiled, knowing that if he didn't see it, he'd hear it in her voice. She touched his arm to reinforce it. "We'll be seeing more of each other, Cliff." She used his name softly but definitely. "When I'm not working at the hospital, my studio is just down the beach."

He nodded, but made no promises.

Then a young man came out of the house and jogged down the path toward them.

"Who's this?" she asked.

Cliff muttered under his breath, knowing his brother Dave would be eyeing the woman with him, asking himself the same question.

Dave obliged by stating it out loud. "And who is this lovely lady?" He was using his smooth-talk voice, or a twenty-year-old's idea of one. "Still picking them up on the beach, bro?"

Cliff cringed.

Dave looked blandly back and forth, but it was obvious he was wondering how much Annie knew about Cliff's disability.

She stuck her hand out for a firm shake. "I'm Annie Rosetti, art therapist at the hospital. We've been chasing after your brother to stop on by for the past week."

"Oh, yeah? Why don't you, big brother?"

Cliff scowled blackly. "This is all I need, nagging at home."

"Could be fun." Dave shrugged. He looked Annie up and down and blushed when he got caught. Just because he was living in his much older brother's bachelor pad on Lake Michigan didn't mean he was nearly as smooth as Cliff when it came to the ladies.

"Are you staying here, Dave?" Annie asked.

"Yeah. Until break is over. Then back to the books."

They chatted. Cliff listened. Annie said goodbye. As she walked off down the beach, Kane dug under the fence post until it was completely revealed.

"She's waving," Dave said to his older brother. He filled in Kane's hole with the toe of his tennis shoe.

"Great."

"Another day, another sunny mood."

"Don't quote Mom."

"Maybe you need one. A mom, I mean."

The good-natured bickering subsided. Cliff let the wind buffet him, listening to the waves crash. Why was he still facing the direction she'd headed as she walked away?

Or maybe he wasn't. How would he know?

He turned toward the house, Dave at his side. "At least you don't run off. The damn dog got away from me and tore up her garden."

"Maybe you should try a cane instead. With a *C*."

"Very funny."

Cliff kicked off his Topsiders on the deck and slid the glass door open. The inside of the house was cool and, as he knew from years of coming here on every available weekend, shadowy and dark compared to the glaring white sand. It had been one of the bigger shocks of the past three weeks to realize that he didn't know this place like the back of his hand; he was still bumping into things.

While Dave gave Kane a fresh bowl of water, Cliff found the couch and mulled over how obvious his first question should be. "So what did she look like?"

Dave snickered. "Wondered how long that would take."

"Think you know me too well, kid."

"Been following you from afar for a long time. Exploit after exploit," he said suggestively.

Cliff lapsed into an imitation brogue he used only in the family. "Mother of mercy, you'd think I wrote home about it."

"I can guess."

"You, kid, have a wild imagination. My sex life is nothing like what you imagine. In fact, it's *all* imagination right now."

"So what about her?"

"That's what I'm asking you. Would she be worth looking up when I can see again?"

"Could be. Is she married?"

"Didn't ask."

"Divorced with four kids and too proud for child support?"

"Didn't ask. She knows I'm blind."

Cliff could almost hear Dave grinning. "So I noticed. You finally told somebody."

"No, I didn't. She knew who I was all along. She tracked me down so I'd take her art class."

"Oh." The disappointment was palpable. "Does she get paid by the student?"

"Thanks for the compliment."

Dave frowned, then gave up on his brother's sarcasm.

Cliff elaborated. "You think that's the only reason a woman would look at me?"

"You didn't see the way she was looking at you."

"Oh, yeah?" The smile was all male.

Dave handed him a can of beer. Cliff knew because he'd heard the hiss of the pop-top all the way across the open living room. The bubbly liquid was cold and strong. He stretched his feet on the coffee table, and Kane flopped, panting, on the floor beside him. He reached down and petted him. Heck, it wasn't the dog's fault that eight months into his puppyhood his master had been rendered useless.

Dave plunked down on the sofa, his heavy feet jarring the table. "Ask her yourself. What she looks like, I mean. See if she's interested."

"And how am I going to do that? Hobble down the beach with a white cane, tapping on doors until I find her cottage?"

"Take her class."

Cliff frowned and muttered something about nagging.

"Might get on her good side," Dave added. "You could score some brownie points for when you can see again."

Cliff downed the second half of his beer and grinned. "Dave?"

"Yeah?"

"Did studying me for twenty years really teach you to be that devious?"

Two

___

Whaddya think, two or three hours?'' Dave opened the car door and escorted his brother to the hospital wing containing Annie's classroom.

"Two should do it. Just drop me here." Cliff shouldered his way through the doors alone.

It was the smell that assaulted him first—disinfectant. Must buy it in fifty-gallon drums, he thought wryly. He felt waxed linoleum beneath his feet, heard nurses in rubber shoes, hushed voices. The memories they evoked weren't pleasant. The oldest ones never ceased to be painful. He had yet to come to terms with the most recent ones.

Three weeks ago he'd woken in a hospital and been told about the explosion in the mine. Something about a faulty charge and a flash, sand particles embedded in his eyes. Bandages had been applied and removed, tests run;

fingers had stretched his eyelids open, shining a penlight at him that looked like the sun behind a heavy cloud.

After two weeks of that sort of treatment combined with unrelenting questioning from the Bureau of Mines people and a half-dozen safety inspectors, all the proper reports had been filed. Meanwhile, the doctors had admitted there was nothing more they could do. They put him on a waiting list for cornea transplants at the University of Michigan and sent him home.

But instead of going to his apartment, he'd chosen the cottage, 150 miles to the south in what was still considered northern Michigan. The local hospital, this hospital, would keep him updated on his waiting-list status.

The first time he stopped by, the staff suggested he learn survival skills by taking therapy classes. But he hated working out on treadmills; they only reminded him of how much better it was running outdoors—fresh air, sunrises. He had no interest in home health care, either. Dave would help him out there. Then they made the mistake of presenting him with a white cane. He broke it across his knee.

Their last suggestion was the art class. Pottery—as if that was a survival skill!

But here he was, listening to the art room fill up: listening to people chatting, electric wheelchairs humming by, a metal walker clicking and scraping across the floor. He'd been escorted to a stool by a nurse. There he sat, restless, vaguely angry, waiting for the class to start. *Let's get on with it*. He didn't give two bits for art he couldn't see. Art for a mining engineer meant graph paper, drafting pencils, computer graphics. What did they call this charade? *Tactile arts?*

But maybe the doctors were right. Maybe it would take his mind off the milky white room he was trapped in. It was like watching people moving behind a linen curtain. Like bandages that never came off.

After a few minutes it was obvious that everyone was waiting for Annie Rosetti. Judging by how quickly he picked out her footsteps as she came through the door, so was he. Hers was the steady go-ahead stride he'd learned on the beach. Today she was wearing sandals, he guessed, flats. Listening to a few more steps, he knew he was right.

Annie wasn't surprised to see Cliff in her class. She'd been warned he was coming. The shock was seeing him smile. Maybe he'd heard her enter. Maybe it was some private thought. It was impossible to tell behind the dark glasses. She tried to feel a twinge of sympathy for his handicap, but she felt absurd feeling sorry for anyone who looked that virile, that mysterious, that just plain dangerous.

Annie smiled. Dangerous? Only to her common sense. He'd probably swallowed some pride to be here. *Because he needs my help,* she reminded herself. That, she would willingly give.

"Class, I'd like to introduce you to our newest member, Cliff Sullivan." He stiffened, she noted, and the smile froze before disappearing completely.

"Cliff, since you can't see, I'll tell you who's here. Emily is on your left. She's in a wheelchair from multiple sclerosis. Bob is to her left, with cerebral palsy. Grant was paralyzed from the chest down in a diving accident."

"Hi," a young man said.

Cliff barely nodded.

"And Susie is on your right. She has arthritis."

"Hi, Cliff." Her voice was very young. Nodding again, Cliff wondered with a pang how young.

"I tell you this," Annie continued, "not because any-one here is identified by his or her disability, but they will be identifiable to you by their sounds. The electric wheelchairs are Emily's and Bob's, Grant uses the hands-on type to keep his muscles looking great—" laughter all around "—and Susie uses the walker. And for your in-formation," she announced, to the other class members, "Cliff is blind."

"Temporarily." It was the first and only word out of his mouth, and already he regretted it. No one else was here temporarily. Just because he didn't belong was no reason to insult people.

Attitude. Annie knew the difference it could make. Grant had adjusted so quickly, modifying his very first wheelchair for racing so that he could remain involved in athletics. Cliff wasn't adapting; he was denying. She had to reach him.

She started with the indirect approach, including him in the group. "Since we have a new member, I get to stand up and give my speech."

Groans and laughter met her announcement. Cliff grimaced but found himself leaning forward for more of her voice. It was the only familiar thing here.

She began, punctuating her words with emphasis. He could almost see her hands darting as her voice rose and fell, fists clenching or fingers pointing. As she moved, he caught a sense of the room's dimensions, never losing track of how far away she was at any given moment.

"I don't care what you can't do," she said. "I want to know what you *can*. And you want to know. That's why you're here. There is something worthwhile in every one of us. Something beautiful. Maybe you don't think so. Maybe others look at the outer shell and see something broken. Don't let anyone judge you by the outside. Show me the inside, what you can *create*."

She moved slowly around the room, laying a hand on a shoulder, touching an arm, her passion and her belief in her work obvious. She approached Cliff last. The closer she got the more suspicion radiated from him. She had one two-hour class in which to gain his trust, to get inside those defenses.

"Some people may dismiss this as mere basket weaving, but I believe in this class. Anything that comes from inside you is beautiful, is worthwhile. Let's get started."

Music began, a salty calypso playing as softly as a Caribbean breeze. Cliff heard the whir of the chairs and people moving past, heard the tinkle of paintbrushes in jars, running water, another page being turned on a drawing pad. Somewhere in the jostle, he lost the sound of her walking.

"Cliff?"

He started and cursed himself. She was right beside him.

"Sorry to startle you." Her voice was warm, her hand resting lightly on his shoulder. "I want to show you this wheel."

She reached around to throw a switch. He heard the potter's wheel start to spin and felt the fabric of her dress sweep and catch against his shirt as she came around behind him.

"This is the clay we'll be using." She plopped a cabbage-sized lump into his hand.

Cliff said the first thing that came into his mind. "Feels like plastique."

"Plasteek?"

"Plastic explosives. Got enough here to blow a good-sized building sky-high."

She laughed lightly. "Well, I've never heard that one before. Tell me more."

He almost did, but it would mean talking about his work, setting charges to loosen tons of rock and ore in the open pit mines of Michigan's Upper Peninsula. It would also mean talking about the explosion. "Just show me what to do with this, Doc."

She settled herself on a stool. "If you could see the getup I'm wearing, you wouldn't think I looked much like a doctor."

"I can hear it. You have bells on?"

"Little Indian bells on the belt, hammered silver. It was made by an artist friend."

Close friend? he wondered. "And bracelets?"

"Always, though they'll come off once we get into the clay. Here, you'll need to wear this." She flapped a cloth in front of him and tried to direct his arms into the smock.

"Oh, no, I'm not." He wasn't about to put on another of those ridiculous hospital gowns.

"You'll get spattered with wet clay."

"I'm not a baby. I don't wear a bib."

"It's an artist's smock."

"No!" The mouth was firm, the jut of his jaw outlined even through the beard. The furrow between his brows was deep and unyielding.

Annie sighed. "Guess it'll have to come out in the wash. By the way, does Dave do that or do you?"

Cliff frowned. Just because he hadn't memorized the washer cycles yet didn't mean it was any of her business. He squeezed the clay so hard it was indented with the shape of his fingers.

Annie wrapped her hands around his and said in a tone of gentle teasing, "You're getting ahead of me, Cliff.

Kneading the clay is next.'' Her fingers threaded with his, pressing softly.

He almost choked. An image of their legs entwined in the same way rocked him to the core. At the same time the smell of her perfume came to him, soft, seductive. He wanted to turn his head and follow that scent to its point of origin, the side of her neck perhaps, or beneath her ear. To put it bluntly, he wanted her. Physically. Immediately.

She continued to touch, to knead, mouthing soft, encouraging words that had his blood racing even while his mind told him what an idiot he was. He was blind. To her he was nothing but a student. If he kept that thought firmly in place, maybe he could get through this thing without making a complete ass of himself.

''All right, teach, what do I do with this useless lump of clay now?''

''Well,'' Annie replied, trying not to sound surprised at his sudden cooperation, ''we center it on the wheel and start it spinning.''

Two hours of hell, that's what Cliff had been through when the music stopped. His shoulders were stiff from hunching over the wheel and his back ached. The concentration needed when one couldn't see was tremendous; a pounding headache was proof of his efforts. But those were only aches and pains.

For two hours he'd had Annie's perfume, Annie's voice, Annie's arms reaching around him, intermingling her fingers with his in that yielding clay, guiding his hands up and down the wet and spinning shape. He'd made two pots, both round and full at the bottom, tapering at the neck. Like a woman. And when she'd shown him how to dip his fingers inside to hollow out the pot, he'd thought he'd break in two.

If this was supposed to relax him, it sure as hell wasn't working. He felt clumsy, tense, helpless and aroused all at once. He felt like a wounded bull in a pottery shop, and Art with a capital *A* wasn't about to assuage him.

Bidding the other students goodbye, Annie watched Cliff get up to leave and sensed every piece of hard-won progress about to slip down the drain. How was he going to get out of here with all those easels and stools in the way? "Cliff? I don't see Dave outside. Why don't you wait a minute while I clean up?"

"No thanks." He had to get out. He kept hearing her swishing around in that dress, that body, that darkness. Every time she walked by he caught the sway of fabric and the sound of bells. What would he do alone with her in this room? Correction, what did he want to do that he was a fool to even dream of?

He was leaving. Now. And he'd be damned if she'd see him shuffle. He took one solid stride and kicked the water bucket next to the potter's wheel. He'd been using it all through class to rinse his hands and moisten clay. He remembered it the moment lukewarm water sloshed over his pant leg and down into his shoe.

He felt like an idiot, and he knew he looked like one. At least the string of curses he let loose was creative. He kicked the bucket halfway across the room.

Annie tossed her smock on the floor. "Damn it, Cliff, I don't tolerate tantrums in class."

"I'm not in your class anymore!" Refusing to mince or hesitate, he stormed forward. Until he hit the wheelchair.

"Hold on a second, man," Grant said, rolling backward, "Let me get out of your way."

"Uh, sorry." He'd thought everyone else was gone.

"Yes, you are sorry," Annie replied tartly, coming up behind him. "You should be. You're also free to leave." Putting the flat of her hand firmly on his back, she steered him on a path through the easels. When there was a straight line to the door, she let go with a slight push for emphasis. "Eight paces, turn left in the hall."

Cliff stopped and turned toward her. To argue, apologize or curse, he couldn't have said. He wanted to break something, hit something, run until his heart pounded like a bass drum in his ears. But no words came, so he walked, hand extended, until he hit the door and slapped it wide open. He executed a neat turn and marched out, quietly calling himself every name in the book. One thing was certain: he was never coming here again.

Dave entered the other end of the hall just in time. "Hey, look out! Stretcher at twelve o'clock."

They looked a lot more like brothers when they frowned, Annie thought, watching from the art room door. Fortunately Dave caught on quickly to her hands-off method. She wasn't helping Cliff because it wasn't the kind of help he'd accept. He'd make it down that hall alone.

He'd do it all alone.

Annie muttered a curse of her own. The man was impossible. Inflexible. His conduct inexcusable.

The hard part was, she could still feel his back under her palm, the slip of fabric against skin as she pushed him out the door, still see his determined walk. It took a lot of courage to walk like that, pretending nothing was wrong, refusing to be slowed down by the simple fact that he couldn't see. Either way he still needed her help. Maybe more than ever.

They would meet again.

Maybe she should add *inevitable* to her list.

* * *

Two days later at 7:00 a.m., watching Cliff jog down the beach with Kane, Annie's plan was made.

She'd been thinking since Tuesday, when the sound of Dave's car had faded outside the hospital and she'd realized she'd been listening to it go. She was determined, too. Cliff had to adjust, to accept himself as he was. But he was proud. She couldn't emphasize his limitations. She'd show him all the things he was still capable of. The months of waiting for his operation would go more easily. And if the operation failed, he'd be that much farther along.

Besides, she knew if she let him simply walk away, he'd haunt her forever.

At the moment it was Kane who was doing the tormenting. Drawn to the water like any Lab, he wanted to play in the waves. No matter how straight a path Cliff maintained, Kane veered to the right with every sixth step. Nikes splashing in the water, Cliff cursed and tugged the dog back as they zigzagged their way down the beach. Annie waited until they were directly across from her house.

"Care if I join you?"

Cliff stopped as if he'd heard a rattler. Actually it was her voice and the sound of bracelets. He steeled himself. "We're heading for the showers. Or the dog pound," he growled.

"Looks like Kane's already had a shower. Hi, beast." She let the overgrown pup slurp her hand. It gave her a moment to take in Cliff's soaked shoes. "Did you two stop for a swim?"

He didn't take kindly to teasing.

She'd been watching them all along, he thought, in which case she already knew damn well they'd been in the water more than out. "I'm not coming back to the hospital."

"I'm not asking you."

He paused, jaw tight. "Then why are you talking to me?"

"I have a proposition."

Not the kind he wanted to hear, he thought.

"I promise you'll never have to come to class again, if..."

"If?"

"If you come to my studio instead. Cliff, Dave's not going to look after you forever."

"I don't need forever."

"You need more than a few weeks. The waiting list could take months, and Dave has to go back to college."

"I'll get by."

"On what? Is he teaching you anything? Or do you blow up every time you hit a snag, until he backs down and does everything himself?"

She'd hit a nerve. Dave wanted friendliness and good times. He'd cater to his brother rather than fight.

"I've had experience, Cliff. I can deal with the anger."

"Is that why you kicked me out of class?"

"You bothered another student. That's not allowed."

"I didn't see him."

They both let that excuse lie.

"I thought they'd all left, that we were alone," Cliff said finally. Thought it, wished it, dreaded it.

"Then the tantrum was for my benefit?"

Yes. It was because of her, because she was a woman he wanted so unreasonably and couldn't have. "It won't work, whatever your proposition is. Kane, home!"

The dog took off in the direction *he* wanted to go, after a flock of sea gulls settling downwind.

"Wrong way," Annie called.

Halting, they came slowly back to the sound of her voice. Sprinkling his request with expletives the dog would never understand, Cliff said, "Just point us in the right direction and drop it, okay?"

"Not okay."

He thought he could hear her folding her arms across her chest, bracelets jangled then muffled, voice tight.

"I can teach you everything you'll need to know when Dave's gone. How to use the can opener, the stove, how to set up the medicine cabinet. Whatever you need for daily living, you'll learn. How to run a washing machine, for instance."

"I know how. I'm not going back to the hospital."

"Accept my proposition and you won't have to. I'm talking about my house. It's better than any classroom. We'll have a real kitchen, real stairs and carpeting."

Kane wanted to stalk the gulls. Cliff let him, following at the other end of the leash. Annie anxiously kept pace, fully aware Cliff hadn't said no.

"And what if I knock over a bucket of dirty water in your living room?"

"My studio is impervious to dirt."

"Your studio is in your house?"

"Semiattached. It's actually a heated garage with concrete floor, a drain and a kiln."

"I could break a lot of pottery, you know."

"I'm not Cliff-proofing my house for your sake. You'll simply have to learn to live with what's there." Annie smiled, a disguised philosophy if she ever heard one.

"So now I'm living there," he said.

"Every day, ten to two. We'll fix lunch, do dishes, run a load of wash, all the things you need to learn. We might even make some pottery. Only catch is, you have to put up with me."

Kane, who had come to a complete halt pointing at the squawking birds, lunged. The gulls scattered and screeched. Cliff reined him in while mulling over Annie's offer.

They'd be spending time together, a lot of it. Alone in a way they'd never be in a classroom. Did this woman have any idea how she was tempting him? On the other hand, maybe she'd never even considered that aspect.

Still breathing hard from the workout with Kane, Cliff was aware of how little he was wearing. The warm southern wind chilled the sweat off his skin, and his nylon running shorts clung to him. He felt on display and there was no way to gauge her reaction. Did she even notice?

He decided it was high time he found out whether she saw him as a student or a man. "If I spend that much time at a woman's place, I usually know a little more about her."

Annie's heartbeat sped up. At least he was thinking about it. She tried to sound cool. "What do you want to know?"

"Starting from absolute scratch, what do you look like?" He looked down at her, those flat black glasses suddenly reflecting her upturned face. With the blunt prickly beard, he could have passed for a dissolute movie star.

Her mouth was suddenly dry. Even though she knew he couldn't see her, his prolonged scrutiny produced the strangest sensation. "Didn't Dave describe me to you?"

Not enough. Cliff didn't reveal how coy his brother had been, suckering him into going to her class. Not that it was Dave's fault anymore—against his better judgment, Cliff wanted to know. He wanted to get out of this self-enclosed prison. He wanted a reaction. "I'd like to see for myself."

Annie had to find her voice first. "All right." She reached out and put her hand on his shoulder so he'd know where she was. Then she touched his chin, tilting it so that he was looking right at her. "I'm directly in front of you."

The minute she took her hand away she wanted to touch his beard again, to feel his shoulder muscles bunch and relax beneath her other hand. She mentally corrected that. What she most wanted was to touch and not get burned. Which was crazy and, with Cliff Sullivan, she sensed, impossible. She clenched her hands at her sides and hoped the tension didn't show in her voice.

"I'm five-five, as you guessed before. You figured out my weight. I have frizzy brown hair that looks like I overperm it."

"Do you?"

"Been that way since I was born. Maybe my mother was frightened by a Brillo pad."

He smiled. "You have some weird ideas."

"Just trying to be honest. I used to do everything but iron my hair to make it behave. Go ahead."

He paused, uncertain, so she lifted his hand.

"You can't see, so touch. Brillo, right?"

He smiled grimly, shaking his head slightly. He patted her hair awkwardly, then pleased himself by catching a strand that was being toyed with by the wind and combed it back in place. This was so intimate, touching a woman's hair. The kind of thing he usually did when pulling a woman toward him to kiss her. He dropped his hand to his side. "All right."

Annie had to swallow, clear her throat, something. Her voice felt as hoarse as his sounded. "Not exactly the classic pageboy," she croaked.

"No."

"I used to dress very understated and preppy."

"Was your family well-off?"

"My husband's was."

"Husband?"

It wasn't something she liked talking about, but she knew he was going by verbal clues alone, so she filled in the details. "Ex-husband. I was the perfect wife while it lasted, or so I thought. Guess I didn't measure up."

"In whose opinion?"

"Ken's."

"And who appointed him God?"

She smiled, then squeezed his shoulder to show she meant it, saying, "Thanks for that one." He was surprisingly easy to talk to, even without visual feedback. He had a very mobile face, little tics, smiles, frowns. "I wish I'd had you around back then. You would've saved me a lot of trouble."

"How so?"

"I've always been what my Mom calls 'artistic.' In her vocabulary that means funky Bohemian clothes made by friends who are into fabric, a lot of jewelry and plenty of color. Needless to say, I wasn't preppy material. Ken wanted to change me, and I wanted to change to keep him. I was so eager to fit in." She sighed, briefly remembering the past. "He left me anyway."

Cliff's face was unreadable. "Must have been tough."

Her shrug took in the sky, the sand, the whole crazy world. She wished he could see it; it was harder to put into words. "We're all stronger than we realize. Trite but true. I know now I'd never have been happy that way. I'm just me now, unapologetic."

She was about to add something, instead she slipped her hand into the crook of his arm and they started walking.

Sometimes she wished she could change back, be as accommodating as she used to be, quick to align her opinion with others'. No more. She was honest and blunt, and her true friends cherished her for that. But some people, she glanced warily up at Cliff, had trouble accepting it. Some men, she reminded herself, wanted a woman more in their own image.

Although they'd lapsed into silence, Annie didn't seem to feel the need to fill it with chitchat. Cliff liked that. He also liked the way she matched him stride for stride. He made sure they kept on the packed sand by the water's edge. That meant she stayed close by his side. She felt good there. Right. Maybe too good. Every now and then the back of her hand stroked his bare waist. That's when he realized his hand had covered hers where it rested in the crook of his arm.

Her perfume was still there, enticingly reaching him whenever the breeze died down. "Your artist friends make clothes and bells and bracelets. Do they make perfume, too?"

His hand was already reaching, catching Annie's nod.

"This one makes potpourri, too," she said, suddenly breathless as he lifted her hair, bending carefully forward to inhale the delicate scent of her neck.

That was accidental, she told herself when his lips skimmed her skin. She tried to breathe shallowly, aware of how dangerously close her breasts were to touching his chest, suddenly aching for just that.

His quick breaths fell on her neck; her eyes fluttered closed. His hand was on her shoulder, steadying her, as if she had any intention of moving. She must be completely crazy. "Cliff."

He turned his head as she turned hers. Chins collided. Embarrassed, he backed away. His hand fell, the backs of his fingers accidentally brushing her breast, discovering the upraised nipple.

For five stultifying seconds nothing was said.

"Uh, sorry," he muttered, color flooding his face.

"You don't have to be embarrassed," she said quietly, as much to herself as him.

"By what?" He pulled his shoulders back.

"Why not be honest?"

"I am," he insisted with a tug on Kane's leash.

"You touched my breast and you're embarrassed, that's what. You're also mad at yourself for doing something dumb."

Mad? He felt mortified, embarrassed and furious. Also as clumsy as a fifteen-year-old at a drive-in. Where was his old suave way with women? Just because he hadn't used it lately shouldn't mean he'd lost it completely. If everything were normal, what would he do in this situation? Try humor.

"You don't have to make up excuses for me, Annie. Where I come from, copping a feel is considered a coup."

"You did that on purpose?"

She didn't sound convinced. All right. As Dave would say, punt. "You didn't describe those to me. It's nice to know who I'm talking to." Lord, that came out crudely. Maybe she'd slap him instead of the pity or revulsion he imagined in her eyes.

Annie was sure Cliff was covering up his embarrassment. She just wasn't *completely* sure. She'd enjoyed his touch. That she shouldn't have, didn't change anything. The memory of the sensation still tingled on her skin, repeating as her breasts rose and fell against the fabric of her dress. The tiny hairs on her neck still prickled.

He was so handsome, so masculine. No matter how she wanted to overlook that for the sake of their relationship, her body wasn't buying.

"Guess private lessons won't work," he said, listening to her silence. His face was immobile, unreadable. Convinced she was embarrassed by this whole scene, Cliff knew exactly where he stood with her. Nowhere.

"May I ask why not?"

"That's obvious," Cliff replied. "I'm too clumsy. And too tempted." He carelessly brushed the back of his fingers over her breast again, surprised at how quickly the nipple hardened. She responded to him. And he could feel his own body responding. Maybe it wasn't a lost cause.

Annie stepped back awkwardly in the soft sand. "We can, we *should* keep this strictly teacher and pupil."

Not on his part, Cliff promised himself silently. He was just beginning to realize how much he needed someone to react to him as a man, to convince him he was just as desirable, just as strong, just as normal as ever. He didn't want her sympathy; he wanted her response. And he was getting it.

He felt his confidence rise. He knew as sure as the sun beating down on his back that she wouldn't buy an outright courtship. She wanted to teach. Okay, he'd go along to get along. Let her teach him Pottery and Dishwashing 101. Meanwhile he'd teach her he was every bit the man he'd always been. And then some.

"Tomorrow at ten, then?"

Annie nodded, rooted to the spot. He touched her arm, his thumb grazing the inside of her elbow, doing strange things to the pulse inside it. "Uh, Cliff, maybe we need some ground rules here."

"Don't pull away," he said softly. "We have no eye contact. This is the only way I can see you."

The request was stated so simply that she couldn't refuse.

"Ten?" he asked again.

His fingers found her cheek and her nod. His touch was gentle, his face impenetrable once more. He turned and followed Kane toward the cottage.

Did he have any idea how she reacted to him? Annie mentally shook herself. She had to keep this professional for his sake. Emotions would get them both mixed up. She was going to help him, and for that, she'd have to gain his trust.

But who was getting close to whom? And who most needed to heed those words of warning?

Three

___

Annie pursed her lips in contemplation, trying to make this piece of clay better, a thinner wall, a more fluid shape. Unfortunately, every time she thought she was onto something, her concentration shifted to Cliff Sullivan.

Willing her hands to be steady as the pot spun, watching thin finger-width notches circling and building, she was aware of how tightly her arms were clamped to her sides, the pressure on the side of her breasts, the sensation, slight, of the nipple he'd touched, hard-tipped and pushing against fabric. A gentle, aching throb. She had a sudden desire to run her fingers across it, but they were clay-smeared.

The pot, its walls too thin, began to cave in.

"Bah!" She shut the wheel off with an angry flick of the switch. Straightening her aching back, she stared purposefully at the shelves of unglazed pots. She had work to do if she was going to be ready for the art fair this weekend. Which one was she scheduled for? It didn't matter; she wouldn't have anything to sell if she didn't get some production going.

"So what about Cliff Sullivan?" she asked the empty room. If their lesson tomorrow went as badly as their art class had, they were doomed to failure.

Used to working with three-dimensional objects, Annie examined the man from another perspective. Obviously he'd been abashed about that touch, at first. Maybe sexual attraction was getting in her way, not his.

At least they'd made some positive steps. She remembered with a flash the first time he'd smiled; she'd been joking about good-looking blond men. But they don't like me, she'd said.

"Words to the wise," she muttered, cramming some clay into a ball and starting over.

The second time he'd relaxed was their walk on the beach, his guessing her height, practically showing off the skills he'd picked up.

Then he'd touched her. In a sense that was good; he was reaching out. He'd found her cheek to check on her nod.

Annie sat up straighter and took a deep breath. There was that sensation in her breasts again, full and tingling. She could blame it on the week of the month, but she knew exactly whose fault it was.

"So he can flirt." She sighed and returned to the analysis. "He knows how. It makes him feel comfortable around me." No doubt that would be the best way to reach him, provided she could take it as lightly as he did.

That was the trick.

Applying patterned indentations to a vase with a small tool, she considered it. By the time she finished, her mouth was as taut as the wire she drew under the clay to separate it from the wheel.

Could she honestly say she wasn't interested?

Yes.

Would she believe it?

No.

She was challenged by the stubbornness in him, drawn to the hurt, attracted to his strength. She'd learned to accept herself exactly as she was. It was taking Cliff Sullivan as much strength, if not more, to deny what he'd become. Contradictory as it might seem, she admired anyone with that kind of courage, the sheer willpower to face reality and say, "No, I won't accept it."

One of the combs loosened in her hair as she bent over to set the vase on the workbench. If she didn't push it back, it might fall and nick her carefully applied pattern. If she did, she'd get clay in her hair. What the heck. She pushed it back anyway. She'd gotten clay in her hair more than once. She wasn't exactly the glamour type.

"And that, Annie Rosetti, is undoubtedly what Mr. Gorgeous is used to."

She'd made a major, painful mistake with her ex-husband, one she didn't want to repeat. Physical attraction was one thing, but you didn't build a relationship on it. Unfortunately some attractive people never learned that. Her ex-husband for one. Cliff Sullivan for another?

Or was she judging him on *his* looks? Seeing through to the inner person was something she firmly believed in. It hurt when you were judged on the surface as she had been judged. And found lacking.

"Cliff wouldn't do that." Cliff was blind; he couldn't. Did that make him safe?

Annie shook her head slowly back and forth. She was applying an awful lot of thought to a man she barely knew. Rinsing her hands off, she pried clay from under her fingernails with an old file.

So what was a woman to do? The answer was surprisingly easy. Help the man. Teach him what she could. After all, he was a student, not a lover.

And she was determined to keep it that way.

The next morning Annie knocked on the glass doors of Cliff's cottage. If she was to regain control of this situation, she had to take the first step.

"Morning, Dave," she called, peering inside.

"Hi. Bring a mop?" he whispered conspiratorially.

"Why? Did he kick over—" Annie stopped with a flinch when she realized it was a joke. At least Cliff had told Dave about the debacle in class. Talking it out might have helped. "Actually, we're going to walk over to my house."

"Come on in. He's upstairs. Classes are at your place now?"

She gave him the address and phone number in case he needed to get in touch during the day, and explained that she was fitting Cliff in prior to her weekday afternoon sessions at the hospital. During the summer months and into the fall, Saturdays and Sundays were reserved for traveling to art fairs.

"You can do that for a living? Don't answer that. Here he is now," Dave announced.

Cliff stopped halfway down the open staircase. Annie swallowed hard. He was wearing cutoff jeans and little else. Droplets of water clung to him from his morning shower. A cotton shirt was slung carelessly over his shoulder. He reminded her of a hunter carting home a lion's pelt. That's when the caffeine from her morning coffee hit all at once, and her pulse set up an erratic hammering.

The frown she recognized from yesterday's class was firmly in place, anchored by glasses as dark as Cliff's mood.

He hated being on display. Who was staring at him now? If Dave didn't speak up, he'd find his kid brother and gladly strangle him.

Then she spoke. "Hi, Cliff."

His stomach contracted at the sound of her voice. She was speaking from the bottom of the stairs; he could almost picture her looking up at him. He pulled the shirt off his shoulder. Slowly. He wasn't going to fiddle with finding which end was which right now. If she liked the view, let her look.

Better yet, let her remember yesterday. Not the art class, but the touch on the beach. He'd had plenty of doubts assault him since the accident, more than a few related to how he'd be perceived as a man. In class, feeling clumsy and buffoonish, with that easy sensuality of hers surrounding him, taunting him, he'd been insecure and frustrated. But it had occurred to him after he'd left the beach yesterday that he'd regained something by touching her, something he wasn't about to lose. She saw him as a man now.

The black mood began to lift. This blindness was a temporary thing. As Dave said, he could lay the groundwork now for winning Annie later. In the meantime he'd be limited to flirting but not following up. That might be its own brand of frustration, but it sure as hell beat loneliness.

Shallow? Maybe. But all the while he'd be subtly winning her. The idea made his whole day.

A slow smile curved his features. "Hello, Annie." His teeth were perfect and white, in two evenly spaced rows. He knew it. Now Annie knew it.

She swallowed, afraid it sounded like more of a gulp in the suddenly silent house. "Hi." She'd already said that.

"So, teach, ready to do it? Your place or mine?" He took the stairs one slow step at a time, grinning as he came.

Annie had that sinking sensation in her stomach again, like falling over a cliff.

Cliff? She blinked. These mood swings of his were throwing her off balance. What was he up to now? Strutting. Sexy. That walk oozed male confidence. Out of the blue, a thought whispered in Annie's ear. Maybe he'd gotten a call from an old girlfriend.

Her heart sank with her smile. Of course. Talking on the phone was something he could do. He wouldn't be blind on the phone; he'd be himself. That would make anyone feel better, put the world back to rights.

Next question, would this old flame pay him a visit?

Or was Annie making it all up? He'd never mentioned— She'd never asked—

She took a deep breath, chased those thoughts out of her head and spoke in her "now, class" voice. She was sure no one noticed the quaver located somewhere near her abdomen. "First thing we're going to do is walk down to my place, counting paces so you can learn the way. When we get there, I'll show you around the kitchen. Then we'll make lunch."

"Lunch? You don't have to do that for me." Cliff ducked his head and scratched his beard with the back of his knuckles, stealing the gesture from a James Dean movie.

Dave's grin was almost loud enough to break the stretching silence. He'd never seen his brother turn it on like this. But the lady was holding her own.

Barely.

Annie recognized twenty-four-karat charm. She might not be impervious to it but that didn't mean she was amused. "You'll be the one doing the cooking, Cliff. You have to learn to do these things by yourself."

He came to a stop at the bottom of the steps and leaned one hip against the railing. "Some things are more fun with two."

Dave choked down a laugh. Whistling a sprightly tune, he suddenly became fascinated with finding Kane's leash as the dog pranced beside the door.

Annie wasn't about to be cowed. "Dave," she emphasized for everyone's benefit, "won't always be here. As for Kane, if he'll behave himself in the house, he can come down the beach with us."

"Oh, *he'll* behave." Cliff smiled, finding the sliding door with little trouble and opening it for her. He stopped on the deck to shrug into the body-fitting knit shirt, grinning wider when his head popped out of the opening, sunglasses still in place. It was as if he'd known she'd be watching. "After you," he said softly.

Every step of the way they silently counted paces. A sound method, it prevented conversation. One look at Cliff's cocky grin and Annie knew there were words that needed to be said; boundaries had to be drawn.

Cliff switched the leash to his other hand so that Kane was on the outside, and casually took her arm. He was whistling the tune he'd picked up from his brother. It didn't help when Annie recognized it as "Na Na Na, Hey Hey, Goodbye." She wasn't about to give up. Or give in.

The tension built with each step. The feel of his fingertips made her keenly aware of the softness of her own skin. Since when was her inner elbow so sensitive? By the time they reached the cottage, her stomach felt as hollow as the wooden deck off her living room sounded.

"Let's just concentrate on the task at hand," she said. That seemed a foolproof path. "You need to operate a can opener first."

"No house tour?"

"Oh, of course." He was right. She'd been so eager to get down to an actual lesson, she hadn't thought of that. And that grin! If he thought he was getting to her, let him believe it. If his touch actually had her picturing showing him the bedroom instead of the living room—

"Can openers! You've got to—"

"Learn this stuff. I know, but, babe—" he laughed softly "—I don't even know where the hell I am yet."

She flushed. Men never called her babe. And if they did, she was sure it wouldn't have that strangely comforting, seductive result. In the meantime her jitters were making a shambles of their first lesson. One thing at a time, Annie. Stick to details. "We're on the living room floor."

"Sounds kinky. But I'm game if you are."

She resoundingly ignored him. "There's a fireplace on the right-hand wall, with a grouping of furniture in front of it. I haven't reorganized anything for your sake, it's all as it was, and it's going to stay that way."

"Is it, now?"

She also ignored the teasing lilt in his question. "As we turn left here, we'll go directly into the kitchen. You can distinguish that by the tile floor." Annie glanced down. He was still barefoot, still had hairy bronze legs like oaks, and those loose-fitting cutoffs were more snug across the front— Her gaze shot back to his face so fast that she could have sued for whiplash.

Tile. Cliff could have recognized it just by Kane's nails clicking as he padded across it. "Okay if I let the dog go?"

"Sure."

Leash unhooked, Kane sauntered to the front door, sniffed the braided rug, circled three times and collapsed with an audible huff, seemingly content to watch the birds and waves for the rest of the morning.

"Don't tell me—he's lying down," Cliff said.

"Right."

"So why is it the world's laziest dog wants to turn every walk into the Boston Marathon?"

Annie shrugged and smiled, unaware for a moment that he couldn't see it. Breathing a prayer of thanks for Kane's interruption, she proceeded with the lesson. "The kitchen is basically two rows of cupboards and appliances on opposite walls, with an eating island in the middle."

"Any hanging copper pots?"

She glanced above the island. "Good point. Yes, a few, and a rack of glasses."

He lifted a hand cautiously above his head and touched crystal. She watched his long, blunt fingers circle a rim. It was dry, no note sounded, except the one deep inside Annie. "Very nice," he said.

Why had she never noticed his voice was so low? "Thank you," she replied.

"Would you like to make lunch?"

That came out sounding entirely too much like something else on her mind.

"Lunch!" She fairly pounced. "Yes, lunch, well, if you'll come down here to the pantry at the end of the counter, we'll get the ingredients."

She described the organization of the shelves, which she *had* rearranged for him: dry goods, napkins and paper towels on top, crackers and cereal on the next shelf, then canned goods, et cetera.

As lessons go, it wasn't too bad. He got the bread out of the breadbox, mayonnaise out of the fridge—confused at first by a pickle jar until he heard the slush of pickle juice—found lettuce in the crisper and set it all out on the island. The can opener for the tuna wasn't too hard, either, except that it required her hands closing over his.

Cliff wasn't about to let that one go. It was as close as she'd let him get since they'd entered the house. "Hands-on teaching, my favorite method." He smiled.

They sat down to eat, Annie choosing a stool on the opposite side of the island. When the meal was almost finished, Cliff saluted her with his beer bottle. "Now that you've wined and dined me, what's next?"

"We clean up."

"Not my ideal way of ending a date." He pursed his lips in a mock pout.

Which only made Annie's eye linger on his lips that much longer. They were moist from the beer. Maybe they tasted of tuna and the saltiness of potato chips. He quirked one side of his mouth, as if aware of her stare. She felt suddenly guilty. "This isn't a date," she said softly but firmly. "I want to teach you."

"That's all?"

"That ought to mean everything to you in the months ahead."

He joined her at the sink to rinse dishes. "Having some company along the way would be nice."

Annie was surprised at how he'd read her thoughts. Company was nice. To her it meant a small circle of friends, easygoing, relaxed, not the tension and zing of awareness she felt every time Cliff was around. That he used every opportunity to bump her, touch her or skim her hands with his while rinsing dishes under running water, didn't help.

But blindness as an excuse only went so far. One look at him told her he wasn't a clumsy man. On the other hand, requesting he keep his distance would be tantamount to admitting he was getting through. She retreated to the island and began to clean off the scraps of food left on her plate.

"I'd appreciate it if you didn't feed him from the table," Cliff said.

Annie looked up in surprise. Of course, he'd probably heard Kane's tags jangle as the dog padded over to where the food was, but there wasn't any way he could have heard her tear off that little piece of crust.

"It's those big brown eyes," he said, smiling grimly. "They'll get you every time." He'd had brown eyes. Before. They appeared milky white now, or so the doctors told him. Not the kind of eyes a woman would want to gaze into.

"Sorry, fella." Annie patted the dog on the head, comparing those imploring eyes to Cliff's sheltered ones. She'd wanted to discourage his flirting, not start him brooding again.

Annie remembered her resolve from yesterday. He was a pupil, so she came up with another task. "Why don't you bring over some laundry tomorrow? You'll need to learn that."

"I know how to do that." His reply was surprisingly brusque, the smile gone as he turned back to the sink.

"Maybe I'm overchallenging you," she said, and immediately bit her tongue. No man would admit to that, especially this one. "I don't want you getting frustrated by learning too many things at once."

"I'm not."

"So what's the problem with laundry?" She hadn't missed his frown.

"I already know how. I've known for years."

"You have to relearn things. I mean, who's going to do your underwear?"

"Who says I wear any?"

"No?" Her mind went blank except for the knowledge that underneath those comfy stretched-in-all-the-right-places cutoffs was more of the bare skin she'd seen this morning. In a way it was a good thing he couldn't see, or she would have been caught staring.

Cliff leaned back against the counter, crossing his arms and those legs, and kept talking. At that moment Annie was grateful for her stunned silence. He didn't offer personal information easily.

"It was a bad habit I got into as a teenager. Not that I do it anymore. When they pulled me out of the mine, I'm sure I was wearing fresh underwear, just like Mom would have wanted."

Annie chuckled. Learning about his past was helpful, but asking about the explosion itself might be too direct. "I bet your mother was upset, after the accident."

"She died, years ago. When Dave was five."

"I'm sorry. How old were you?"

"Nineteen. She was in and out of the hospital for a number of years before that. My assignment was always laundry. I figured out pretty quick to wear as little as

possible, for as many days in a row as I could manage."
Cliff chuckled this time. "When the going gets tough, the
tough minimize."

"I haven't heard that one before."

"Personal philosophy of mine." He took a step toward the island, found his beer with a motion like
sweeping crumbs off the Formica, and swallowed the last
of it. "It was a bad time, especially her first few operations. Dad was working extra shifts and didn't know
what to do with two boys at home. We all handled it as
best we could. I cut a lot of classes, quit a couple of
sports, baby-sat Dave and took it day by day. You travel
light when you have to travel fast."

Annie didn't wonder that he kept so much to himself.
As a teenager he'd gone from a normal home to complete disruption of his family life. Almost four weeks ago
he'd gone from seeing to not seeing in seconds. So he was
traveling light, letting no one near. What was his philosophy, 'When the going gets tough, the tough minimize'?
Yes, she thought, and they hold it all inside.

She came around the island to touch his arm. "I'm
sorry I asked, but thank you for telling me."

He grinned slightly and cocked his head. "Anytime."
Standing so close, it wasn't hard for him to reach up and
find her cheek. Sliding the backs of his fingers over her
skin, he thought he felt that fine peach fuzz women have.
He never remembered his fingers being that sensitive. His
thumb stroked her lips, the lower one full, the tiny row
of teeth behind.

His fingertips were wet, slippery from the soap. Dia-
mondlike bubbles caught the light and dissolved in his
palm. As he traced her cheekbone, Annie felt the cool
trail of water where his breath met streaks of wetness.

For a searing instant she envied him the ability to narrow everything down to touch. If only she could touch his beard the way he was touching her cheek, or his lips the way he was running his fingers over hers. She had the sudden urge to dart her tongue out and lick the moisture off the tip of his thumb. "Please," she breathed.

"All you had to do was ask," he replied seductively.

"That's not what I meant."

"No?" A wry smile was his only reply to her haltingly spoken words. As far as he was concerned, he knew exactly what she meant.

Annie shook her head, momentarily dislodging his hand. It was soon back, palm to cheek, so gentle she wanted to stay right there and nuzzle against it. This time the word, "Don't," came out, slightly shaky.

"I never force, Annie." His hand slipped down her cheek and found the pulse in her neck, pounding slowly against the slight pressure of his massaging thumb. Her head tilted, her shoulder rose. She liked that. She also liked his fingertips tracing her collarbone through the filmy cotton dress. And when he got to her breast, a warm handful with a nubbing peak . . . "You only have to ask," he repeated softly.

She wanted to ask, ask for things she had no right even imagining. Things that had nothing to do with her helping him, more like him pleasuring her. Her eyes had fluttered shut. They snapped open. "No!" She stepped back, startled by the sensations that rocked her as his thumb did something delicious to her left breast.

"I was under the impression I could touch anything I could identify. Isn't that part of our lesson?"

This time she slapped his hand down. Anger was easier. "Now you're being purposely obnoxious."

"And aren't you being a bit of a tease?"

"This won't help you."

"Wanna bet?"

"It will interfere with what I'm trying to teach you."

"Teach me." He touched her waist, making her insides feel as quivering and airy as soap bubbles. "Teach me, Annie," he repeated more strongly, an air of desperation in his words.

There was so much he wanted to be. How could she deny him the chance to be a man again? "Cliff, you can have everything you had before. Believe me. The accident hasn't made you any less attractive."

"Then come here."

His hands closing on the bare skin of her arms was like the first blast of shower spray in the morning. She had to brace herself for it.

He felt her stiffen. "I can have women. I just can't have you. Is that it? And how am I supposed to meet these women?"

"So you want me because I'm available." It was the perfect opportunity to take offense. Annie used it.

"I want you period, damn it. And don't run away! I need to touch you when I talk to you, otherwise how do I know where you are?" He ran his hand over her cheek again. "I can't tell if you're stifling a yawn or rolling your eyes."

"You can't touch everyone you talk to."

"No, but I need to touch you."

Annie felt a pang. Here she was so busy protecting herself that she was forgetting her duty to him. It took guts to admit need like that, especially for someone as determined to go it alone as Cliff. It was a step she had to acknowledge. "I'm here," she said, touching his face in return.

Now they were getting somewhere. Cliff flinched at how self-centered his words sounded. Annie was being helpful, sensible. And he was acting like some randy teenager, trying to gain control over this crazy situation by being macho, wanting her to dance to his tune, to prove he was still good for something. "I'm sorry," he mumbled.

He found his way to the kitchen island and whistled for Kane. With one hand under the dog's collar, the other searched for the leash coiled on a chair.

"You don't have to go," she said, her voice husky and soft.

"I'm doing this all wrong. You should have kicked me out ten minutes ago."

"We can keep this professional, you know."

"Not if you keep doing that."

He motioned downward with his chin, and Annie realized her hand was on his chest, fingertip inches away from the hair that coiled at the open V-neck. "Sorry."

"You want me to be a student instead of a man," he said, not yet resigned to playing by her rules.

"You haven't stopped being a man, Cliff. Believe me."

She didn't have to touch him; her voice did it for her, soft, concerned, keeping him rooted when he knew he'd be better off leaving. It was the way she paused when she used his name, making him picture her mouth, her teeth touching her lower lip, coming to rest there. Were those lips moist, or dry and slightly parted?

He could drag her to him and kiss her until there was no doubts. His tongue forging into her mouth, her lips forming themselves around it, her body moulded to his.

The only thing stopping him was the fact that he didn't know exactly where she was.

Or what she looked like.

Or how she might be looking at him at this very moment.

Who was he kidding?

"All right," he said stiffly, "I won't bother you anymore. You're the teacher. I'm the pupil."

He'd stay with it, if only to hear her say his name a few dozen more times. He'd risk her stray touches, her determined concern. Whether the lessons worked or not didn't matter to Cliff anymore. He got the distinct feeling that around Annie Rosetti the most important lesson he'd learn was just how far his self-control stretched.

"Thank you," Annie said, but the words lacked enthusiasm. He was saying what she wanted to hear, but his abrupt mood change made her feel like an emotional elevator ride had come to a sudden, bumping halt.

Four

___

The dark Cliff was back, Annie noticed as they crossed through the kitchen for the next day's lesson. *The Dark Cliff* sounded like some kind of Gothic novel, she thought, trying to work up a smile. The tension that entered the house with him didn't allow for more than a mirthless smirk.

"This door leads outside," she began, taking him through the kitchen. "There's a flagstone path, as you can tell."

"I can feel it."

Because he was so heedless of obstacles, barging ahead, she kept a lookout for anything he might bump into. "Good. Six paces and you'll be at the garage door."

"Got a lawn mower needs fixing?"

She laughed, or tried to. That didn't come out right, either. Although they were supposed to be on formal terms, his withdrawal bothered her more than ever. Was it because she'd drawn lines when he'd tried to reach out yesterday? No going back now. "This is my studio. I like it separate from the house because of the kiln."

Kane trotted in as they entered, nose to the concrete, tail wagging as he circled the room.

Cliff just stood in the doorway. "He won't knock anything over, will he?"

"No, he's fine. Will he stay if we open the garage doors? I'll be firing the kiln and it gets stuffy in here."

"He'd better," Cliff growled. "Kane! Sit."

Annie had to guide Cliff's hand to the garage door latch. "We'll lift together, but be careful. It sticks in the middle."

With one heft the door swung upward so fast that it clanged against the rail stop and bounced back. Pulled off balance, they brushed against each other, only inches apart, as they listened to the clang fade in the big room. She could smell his cologne. No, it was something subtler—a spicy soap.

"That was easy," she said, trying to sound encouraging instead of nervous.

A breeze blew in and a jangle of sound surrounded them.

"What's that?"

"Chimes," she replied, fixing a comb in her hair.

"You collect them?"

"I practically live off them. They're my best sellers. It's a basic pot shape turned upside down, with hanging elements made from cookie cutouts or long painted strips of clay."

"Let me see."

She took his hand, leading him past sawhorses with plywood tops that stood in for tables where numerous pots were drying.

Following the remaining tinkling sound, Cliff reached up. Touching dangling strips, he felt the rasp of rough clay on one side, smooth glaze and slightly raised paint on the other.

And he felt her hand. It fitted his perfectly, firm, good-sized, not callused, but not flimsy, either. He ran his thumb absently across her fingertips.

It was a moment before Annie noticed. She was watching his face relax at the bell-like sounds. His head tilted back, and she took in his strong neck, the mixture of blond and brown hairs in his beard.

"These sound the way you smell," he said softly.

He could tell by the sound of her indrawn breath that her lips had parted. She wanted to say something, he knew, but she had to think it through first. This was going to be harder than he thought. He'd told her he wouldn't bother her anymore, but she wasn't about to give him the same distance, let him crawl off to some cave and lick his wounds. Not Annie. She wanted to help. She wanted in. So did he.

He abruptly let go of her hand and listened to her retreat to what sounded like a wooden chair scraping on the concrete.

"Ninety-degree turn to your left, three paces, and you'll find a chair to sit down on," she said in her businesslike manner.

Cliff found the chair and sat, legs out, crossed at the ankles. He wore khaki shorts and a navy blue polo shirt.

Downright formal for him, Annie thought wistfully, preparing her glazes. That was how it would have to be if she had any hope of teaching him things he didn't already know. But how did you teach someone to live again? How did you grade it?

If there was a grade for being aware of him as a man, she'd be valedictorian by now. She noted where his shirt sleeve ended and his biceps began, how the nubs of his nipples pressed against his shirt. Did it mean what it meant on a woman? Was it the same as the way her body reacted when she thought of his touch?

"So you don't just teach," he said, scratching aimlessly at his chin. "You sell these things?"

She took a deep breath and dispelled the images that looking at his body created. At least someone had the sense to make common conversation. "Pottery is my main source of income, although teaching is more regular. I work the art fair circuit in the summer, teach an adult education class at the community college in the winter, therapy classes year-round. Mornings I work in here, catching up on my inventory."

"Sounds very professional."

"Gotta earn enough to keep me in clay and paint." She tried to sound bright and nonchalant. It fell flat.

He wasn't smiling, he wasn't teasing, he wasn't flirting. He was remote. He was waiting for something, some sign from her. One she couldn't give.

Cliff listened to her puttering around a while longer. He wanted the wind to blow, more chimes to sound. There was something magical, something of her in them, saying things she was too cautious to say. Or so he'd like to think. "What are you doing?"

"I'm firing up the kiln."

"Anything I can do?"

She had to be honest. "Actually, not much right now."

You can say that again, he thought.

Annie was still talking. "This part is mostly visual. I'm doing a little handpainting and glazing while the others are fired."

She tried to work and watch him at the same time, the hair on his arms, the sturdy legs, the tapping foot betraying his restlessness.

The chimes rang, and he turned and listened. Kane lifted his nose to sniff the air but didn't move from his chosen spot on the cool concrete. They got through another few minutes.

"What are you doing now?" he asked.

"Putting this one in the kiln."

He heard the rumble and hiss of the heat. He'd never noticed heat had a sound before and the smell of it, dry and powdery, made his nostrils twitch and distend.

She closed the heavy door with a thud and set a timer to ticking.

"My eyes are fine," Cliff said, apropos of nothing. Maybe that was what she was wondering. Maybe it was holding her back. Fear of his appearance without the glasses might be a shallow reason, but it was understandably human, easily forgivable.

"They're milky-looking, so I've been told. They'll be normal again after the operation. Brown."

"Oh."

His jaw was tight, his fist clenched on his thigh. He scratched his beard until she thought it would rub off. She wanted to get these pieces finished before lunch, but he was feeling useless and she was spending half her time watching him. "Would you like to do something?"

"Such as?" His voice was soft, his face relaxing briefly, a flash of bittersweet smile.

Annie's stomach dipped. No, she hadn't meant that. She thought they'd come to some sort of agreement. So far he'd respected it, although it was costing him every minute he sat there. "I meant something useful. You look bored."

Bored? *Honey, I'm set, wired and ready to explode,* he thought wryly.

"How about lunch? You breezed through it so easily yesterday, I thought you could try it on your own today."

Cliff thought of a couple other things he'd been doing on his own lately. "Right. Lunch." He was up and out of his chair and through the door.

Annie sighed and combed her thick hair with her fingers. She never ceased to marvel at how he walked, betraying no hesitation about where he was going. Guts. Pride. When he knew his way, you'd never guess he was blind.

He found the garage's side door and slammed it, the kitchen door and slammed it, and now he was banging around in the pantry setting ingredients on the counter with a thud. All of it without a speck of assistance from her. As a teacher, she should have been proud of herself.

"Damn proud," she muttered, forcing herself to concentrate on one more pot.

Suddenly she realized Kane was standing, the hair on his back upright, body quivering.

"What is it, boy?"

Her eyes followed his. A chipmunk was standing in the woodpile, frozen in place. The animals were at a standoff.

"Now, Kane," Annie said soothingly, "you don't need a snack that size...." Rising from her bench, she approached cautiously. If she could get his collar before—

Too late. With a series of ferocious barks and madly waving tail, Kane gave chase. The chipmunk dashed through the woodpile, out the other side and was lost in a tiny flurry of dead leaves and downed twigs.

"Kane!"

There was a crash in the kitchen.

"Cliff!"

Annie raced to the kitchen to find a jar of pickles shattered, a can of tuna hanging from the can opener, Cliff holding a bleeding thumb, and the roll of paper towels unrolling across the counter and onto the floor, where at least ten sheets were soaking up the mess.

Cliff launched into a full-length, expletive-packed explanation ending with, *"And what's that blasted dog barking about?"*

"He's chasing a chipmunk!" she shouted back. "I'll bandage your thumb, then we'll go look for him."

"What do you mean we'll look? Is that some kind of sick joke?"

"He'll come when you call."

"If he did, he'd be a better trained dog. Let's go."

"I have to bandage this!"

"I'll live!"

Why were they both shouting at the tops of their lungs? Annie took a calming breath and held his hand under running water. "It doesn't look deep, but it's jagged. He sounds like he's getting closer."

"Maybe somebody will mistake him for a bear and put him out of my misery."

"That's not funny. He's a faithful friend, and if he goes a quarter mile farther, he'll be out to the main road."

"He doesn't have the brains God gave that chipmunk, and if he finds the road as often as he spots my house, we've got nothing to worry about."

They made it as far as the garage where Cliff stopped, asked how close the neighbors were, then let loose a string of curses Annie hadn't heard from him even in art class, each of which began with, "Kane, you worthless..." He then put two fingers in his mouth and whistled three short blasts. The barking stopped.

In a matter of minutes the dog came trotting through the underbrush, panting heavily, covered with burrs, and grinning to beat the band. He circled Cliff once, then sat at his feet. Cliff had only to reach down to pet him. "Your hunting luck must be as rotten as mine, pal."

Surprisingly the next three weeks went more smoothly. They settled into a routine of lunch, laundry and the housecleaning tasks Cliff would need to manage the basics—making beds, vacuuming, dishes. Although his progress was rapid, Annie didn't want to build too fast.

There were still things he refused to bow to. He walked way too fast, and Annie winced every time he banged a shin. When she removed the coffee table to another room, he insisted she put it back. All part of denial, his refusal to live within his limitations. Annie had yet to teach him that the most important lesson of all was accepting himself as he was.

When a rare free weekend came along at the end of August, Annie decided to put it to good use. She'd show Cliff that life, as is, was worth living. There could be fun as well as lessons. With certain reservations, he could do many of the things he used to.

Cliff packed the lunch and Dave drove them to the marina in Leland where Cliff's speedboat had been docked all summer.

"One small question," Annie asked after Dave had helped them both into the boat. "How do you start one of these things?"

Dave crouched on the dock above them. "Well, you see that key—"

The engine roared and bucked to life.

"Then there's the throttle...no there. Yeah, that. You pull back on that—"

The engine sputtered, choked and died. A thin film of gasoline leaked out into the water.

"You gotta pull back on it a little faster. Here—no, wait."

"Dave, stay out of the boat," Cliff ordered. "Let me handle that." Hands on her shoulders, Cliff firmly moved Annie aside and started the boat himself.

"Hey, great." Dave sunk his hands in his pockets and stood grinning. "You're teaching him a lot."

Cliff spoke before Annie could. "I didn't take you and your friends waterskiing for six summers without knowing how to start a damn boat."

"Now if you could work on his manners," Dave added.

"I'm afraid that's a lost cause." Annie laughed. "We ready to go?"

"Just don't let him back it out of the slip. The marina would have a fit."

"Cliff, how about if I steer—"

But Cliff wasn't about to relinquish the wheel. "Just tell me where to point it. Dave, cast off!"

Annie caught the rope and Dave's attention as the boat puttered away from the dock. He merely shrugged and rolled his eyes. A lot of help he was.

"Tell me when we hit open water." Cliff couldn't hide the beginnings of a grin.

"I won't have to tell you if we hit anything else. This has to be illegal."

"Who's to know I can't see? Everybody on this marina's wearing shades."

"True," she murmured between clenched teeth, standing beside him at the wheel. "Stay to the right here."

"Starboard."

"Aye-aye."

The idea had been to get him into the open air, to do some of the things he used to, to show him life didn't have to be reduced to staying in your house or walking down the beach just because you couldn't see.

Instead, she was in a speedboat being piloted by a blind man! She had to be crazy. Maybe that explained her laughter floating across the wind as they reached the marina opening and Cliff, after checking with her about incoming traffic, revved the engine to maximum speed and headed out into Lake Michigan.

"Wide open," he shouted, putting down the throttle and lifting his chin above the slanted windshield. The wind rustled his hair and whipped through Annie's. She grabbed a ribbon from her purse and tied her hair in an impromptu ponytail.

"How far are we going?" she shouted.

"How about Wisconsin?"

Her laughter ran up and down Cliff's libido, but the wind was great, the speed greater. God, he'd missed this, and he had Annie to thank. He pulled her to him for a quick hug.

Annie glanced up at him. With the wind in his hair, those shades and that scruffy beard, he looked like a cross between a *Miami Vice* cop and a pirate racing off with his treasure. For a sudden, piercing moment she wished that could be true.

"Maybe I should go sit in back," she said.

"Who's going to watch for innocent civilians?"

"There's no one for miles."

A full-blown smile broke through. "Just what I wanted to hear." He spun the wheel hard right, and she tumbled against his side, clamped there by a strong arm. "Oops," he lied.

But she stayed, one arm holding on to his waist. He knew she could feel the muscles there, expanding with his breathing, the pinery scent of his soap, which came to him on the same breeze that brought her perfume, the rasp of his shirt against hers as they bounced over the waves. For the moment he enjoyed nothing more than that.

Soon a sheen of cool spray lightly covered them. Cliff could feel the blue skies and deeper blue water in the noise, the roar and the splash. The aroma of gasoline grew fainter, the air fresher, and Annie's perfume— He dipped his head to see if he could smell it again. She stiffened, but she didn't say no. School was out. This whole day was a distraction, and he meant to make the most of it.

The boat cut across a series of waves, jarring them both.

"What was that?"

"The wake from a freighter."

He knew she was joking. The bouncing gave him an excuse to move his hand up and down her back.

She had on a loose cotton shirt, like a man's. His palm itched to find out how low it hung. Did it just cover her derriere? Did the tail end flutter around her thighs? His hand strayed as far south as his thoughts.

"Cliff." Annie tried to push off, splaying her fingers ineffectively against his knit shirt and the muscles beneath.

"What's wrong? There aren't any boats around."

"What if I told you that freighter is about to mow us down?"

He killed the throttle right there and the boat came to a rocking halt, her body once again balanced against his. "Then give me a last kiss."

What Annie had dismissed as vibrations from the boat didn't stop with the engines. She backed out of his arms. "Maybe we should have lunch instead."

He grinned and held his hands wide in a gesture of surrender.

Except for the waves slapping hollowly against the fiberglass hull, the day was still. She opened the cooler while Cliff took a bench seat along one side. Kneeling in the center of the boat, she tried not to notice the gap where his cutoffs ended, where she could follow the hair on his thighs so far up.

Who had she been kidding when she'd promised them a day to relax? She was miles into Lake Michigan with a virile, frustrated man. If she thought they'd be safe because they were out of the pressure cooker her house had become...

A glistening can of beer slipped through her hand and rolled across the floor.

Cliff followed the sound of the roll and found it. Coming back to his seat, his leg brushed her thigh.

"You're going to have to sit," Annie said. "There's no room for both of us down here."

She steadfastly ignored his quiet "Oh, yeah?" But her nerves didn't.

"Your sandwich," she said bluntly.

He recognized that tone. It meant he was getting out of line. Good. She'd noticed. He'd been in line entirely too long. He stuck his hand out for the sandwich. "I'll behave. Is this my beer?'' He raised the one he'd picked up.

"Sure.''

He popped the top.

"Yeow!'' Annie jumped at the shower of ice-cold beer. "That's freezing!''

"Hope you like domestic,'' he said, laughing.

"You did that on purpose!''

"I didn't aim it, did I? Look, Annie, it's been bobbing all this way. It's bound to be shook up.''

Annie knew exactly how it felt.

"Want me to dry you off?'' he asked, leering.

"Only if you want to get snapped with a towel!''

"Getting kinky again, but I'm game. Oh-oh, I can hear that glare from here.'' He hefted the half-empty can to measure its contents. "You must be soaked. Tell you what. Take your shirt off, rinse it in the lake, then spread it on the windshield to dry.''

His suggestion sounded so practical that she couldn't argue. Still, she made no move.

"If you take off yours, I'll take off mine,'' he offered, stripping with one quick overhead motion and ducking his head to prevent dislodging his glasses. Then he sat back, his arms stretched across the back of the seat, emphasizing his bare chest.

He had to be doing that on purpose, Annie thought.

"Amazing how hot it gets when you stop moving.'' He stretched his legs halfway across the boat.

His chest rose and fell. Some hairs were dark, some bleached against gold; he'd been lying out in the sun. She wondered where the tan ended and the tan line began. Maybe it was that vivid picture that made her feel downright wanton standing before him unbuttoning her shirt.

Fortunately the chilly water she rinsed it in got her mind off bodies for a moment. She stepped over Cliff's feet to get to the windshield to hang the shirt up. There was a pulse pounding slowly in his bicep. She could see it. Could he feel it?

He slouched further for maximum sun and patted the seat beside him. "Come eat your lunch."

The way her pulse skittered he might have said, "Come *meet* your lunch." Annie perched dutifully on the far edge of the seat.

He grinned and scratched his beard, and her heart fluttered like a landed fish. Funny that she should be having trouble breathing, what with all this fresh air. The vinyl seat made a squeaking noise as she squirmed.

"Tell me more about this ex-husband of yours."

She raised her eyebrows, but the look did him no good. Annie realized she'd have to respond to the question. "That's very specific, isn't it?"

He shrugged. " 'Tell me more about yourself' seemed too pat."

"Easier to answer."

"With pat answers." He downed the rest of his beer, frowning. Maybe he was going about this all wrong. It was so hard to gauge her reactions when he was literally in the dark.

The pause gave Annie an excuse to fumble in the cooler for another beer. "Be careful opening this one."

"Was it the wrong question?" he asked cautiously. "I'm sorry if I'm prying—"

"No, it's not that. It's painful."

"Not the great love of your life?"

"I've been in love before," she said, sitting beside him again. "I'm sure I will be again. It just gets a little harder each time."

"Scar tissue," he replied quietly.

She smiled in response to his gentle grin. He was very sensitive sometimes. It didn't gibe with the cavalier image he tried to project. "Have you been married?"

He shook his head. "I lived with a woman until I moved to the Upper Peninsula. It's remote up there, and she didn't want to move."

"That's too bad."

"She helped me pack the U-Haul."

"Nice of her."

The muscle in his jaw tensed and relaxed, covered by a beard that was filling in more densely every day. It looked like mink. Annie wanted to comb it with her fingers, running against the grain. She closed her hand around the beer can.

"I thought that one would work out," Cliff said, still lost in thought.

"That one? How many others?" she asked lightly.

He laughed out loud. "Hundreds! Very tactful, Annie."

"You do give the impression that there were dozens, at least."

"I do?" He would have looked at her then if he could have. At least those occasions when he played the flirt had worked. She knew he was capable. "Let me see if I can count them all...." Mouthing the numbers, he ticked off each finger, then crossed one ankle over his knee to count his toes.

Long, bony, masculine toes, Annie noticed, sprinkled with dark brown hair. He had a high arch, blue veins. She'd never thought of toes as particularly sexy. Which was why she was surprised to picture herself massaging that arch, washing those toes one by one.

Finishing with his other foot, Cliff grumbled, "I'm running out of digits."

Annie snorted. He was making fun of her. "You need a calculator for all your conquests?"

He leaned over to slip his Topsiders back on, and found her ankle. "Aha. The numbers above twenty." Sitting Indian style on the deck, he counted each of her toes, starting with the littlest, small and humpbacked. Then the next, the pad of his finger covering the pink-polished toenail, his thumb on the underside, making her toes involuntarily curl around it.

"That tickles."

"Shh. Don't make me lose count. I'll have to start over. This is Cissy, and this was Virginia, and this was Valencia..."

Annie was laughing so hard that she hiccuped. "That is *not* Valencia!"

"Funny, they kind of blur after a while."

He still hadn't answered her question—*how many others?* "You like women. I get the point."

"Nothing else like them," he replied lightly. His fingers found the bones radiating from her toes to her ankle. He wasn't surprised he could circle that ankle with one hand. "That doesn't mean I'm the playboy you think I am."

If he wasn't, he'd certainly learned somewhere. She'd heard of feeling something down to your toes, but what happened when it started there?

"Sure, I was kind of wild in college," he continued, massaging her Achilles tendon, working his way up her calf. "I'd been housemother to Dave for so many years, I was ready to break out. Girls were fun. They looked after me for a change. But when Linda wouldn't come North with me, maybe it was the scar tissue thing." His hand stopped. "I settled down and stopped looking for a while."

"Completely?"

He shrugged, running his hand through his hair. "I always assumed I'd get around to meeting someone." Then the accident happened. What if the next twenty years were as empty as the past three had been?

Cliff sat up straight. He'd wasted enough time. "What do you think of me, Annie?"

He waited for her reply, listening with every nerve in his body. Annie suddenly wished they could go back to the playfulness of a moment ago. Instead she got up and went to the front of the boat. "You know I don't think it's a good idea, getting involved now."

"No?" He grinned, or tried to. There was a furrow between his brows that showed he was taking her answer very seriously.

"I want to help you."

"You have."

She could see that it wasn't what he wanted to hear. "I think getting involved would interfere with that."

He walked toward her, cautiously for once, feeling for the break in the breeze where her body was. "And if I learn my lessons like a good boy?"

He was angry. He didn't want to win her by behaving. Rewards for performance. An apple for the teacher. He wanted real life, getting close to someone who understood him. That meant Annie. She put up with him, excited him, and although she kept denying it, she responded every time he came near.

He moved in closer, blocking her body against the captain's chair. Let her deny this.

"Cliff, this could ruin everything we've built."

"We could have more." He pulled her to him, legs to legs, waist to waist, her breasts against his chest. He might be six inches taller, but every inch of them matched.

"Don't," she pleaded in that breathy voice.

"Did you know you make me feel like the sexiest man on earth when you do that?"

She trembled. The desire between them was hard and pronounced. The boat swayed as if they were dancing.

"I'm a man, Annie. Treat me like one."

She didn't want to. The student she could handle; the man made her weak and dizzy and ready for anything. She struggled.

"Afraid of me?" he whispered.

"No."

His voice dropped with his hands. "Is it because I'm not a threat?"

"No."

"Do you have another lover?"

"No."

"A sensual woman like you with no one? Maybe you're using up all your caring on people who can't return it. Students you won't let get close—"

"I'm not afraid." But her tongue felt papery and dry until his head dipped, came closer, and their lips met.

She'd seen that coming, even tilted her head for him. Why did it shock her? Like lightning finding a lightning rod. Her hands were limp at her sides, but her mouth was his to plunder. He probed, she took. He sucked, she gave. A moan escaped but got no further than his mouth.

He spread his hand on her naked waist until his little finger touched her bikini bottom, his thumb the top half. He traced the lower edge of her breast and found a bow between them. He tugged. It didn't untie.

That's when his mouth released hers, his voice harsh. "What color?"

"Blue."

"Look good on you?" He put his hand on her bare skin again. It quivered. So did he.

"Yes," she said.

His mouth was inches from hers. "Say that again?"

She cleared her throat, anticipating, hoping. "Yes."

"That's what I thought you said."

His mouth covered hers, slowly. He didn't want to think about how long it had been, how many times he'd imagined what he couldn't have. Her lips were moist but closed. He didn't need them to open right away, not this time. Now while there were a hundred other things he could feel—her breasts in the Lycra suit, full and heavy, just touching his chest. Did they press over the top of it? His hands would have to find out. That too could wait.

There were still her knees to feel, brushing his legs, her thighs, smooth, ruffling the hair on his as he spread them to draw her closer. She hesitated.

"I want the bare skin between here." He touched her bikini bottom. "And here." He touched the top. "Pressed here." He rubbed her hands across the rippled muscles of his abdomen and stretched them around his back. That brought her hips in contact with his. "I want you to feel everything you're doing to me."

Not as obvious but just as potent was what he was doing to her. She felt milky, melting, rolling inside like the waves. Her knees were weak, or was it the motion of the boat? "Cliff this is going too fast."

"Do you know what I want?"

She didn't dare say.

"Put your tongue in my mouth."

Five

Annie couldn't breathe. Her eyes opened and his face was there, dark, brazen. Her eyes closed and she couldn't escape. Tumbling, falling sensations she couldn't deny. She let him fill her with his tongue.

Never had she felt so surrounded, speared. His beard scratched her chin, too long to be stubble, too thick to be soft. It was like a camel hair brush, stiff from one angle, erotic and silky from another. He brushed her cheek with it, her neck, the cleft between her breasts.

His lips tugged the bow on her bikini. She felt that tug to her toes and back again. He was holding her, he was hard, was there anything happening that she hadn't wished for these past three weeks? Was there any reason they couldn't just keep going, ignoring who they were, what she was to him? She wanted to show him life could still be lived. But what price would she pay for that lesson? Although her mind fought it, her body had long since surrendered.

Cliff felt her growing hunger. She stroked his chest with the flat of her palm, one hand tangled in his hair, tearing a ragged groan from him.

Her body, voluptuous and warm, sidled against his in a shimmy he didn't have to see to appreciate. He felt it the length of his manhood. He heard it as he tugged one breast free of her bikini, handling it like precious gold, kissing it, rasping it with his tongue, vainly trying to fill his mouth with it.

There was something in her he needed desperately. She believed in him, as he was, saw him at his weakest and didn't turn away. For her sake he wanted to be as good as he'd ever been, confident, strong, sure. He reached around her back, fumbling with the bikini's catch.

"Let me," she said.

"I can get it," he replied hoarsely. He didn't. The catch eluded him again. He cursed to fill the silence.

"It's okay, Cliff." She reached behind her, but he was already stepping back.

"Never mind."

In the cool air suddenly separating them, Annie watched him walk back to his seat. She covered her breasts with her arms, swallowing the taste of him still on her tongue. "Talk to me," she said, louder than necessary. "Don't hide behind those glasses."

He shook his head roughly. What was he feeling guilty for? If he couldn't see the hurt in her eyes, how did he recognize the hurt in her voice? He cursed. They couldn't build any kind of relationship on this. She'd been telling him that all along. Why hadn't he listened?

"I could say you owe me an explanation," she said, her voice steadier.

"What do you want from me, Annie? Some high school kid fumbling his way through an idiotic parody of lovemaking? I haven't been this clumsy since I was seventeen."

"It's always awkward the first time. People need to learn each other."

"Very wise," he answered with a laugh. "When they can see, maybe. We both deserve better. I'm sorry I got out of line."

The sea gulls overhead mocked and cawed.

Annie rearranged her bikini and plucked her shirt off the windshield. It was almost dry. For some reason she wanted to wrap as many layers around her as she could. They were flimsy armor; the hurt had already been done.

Speckles of sweat on her neck cooled in the breeze. Or was that moisture from his kiss? She shivered and buttoned one button at a time, refusing to let her hands shake.

"This was a kind of first for you," she said. "I'm sorry. I should have been more sensitive to that."

"For Christ's sake, don't apologize!" he exploded. "I'm a man, Annie. I won't be less."

"I don't want less."

He hadn't meant to hurt her. He'd been up and down and angry as hell the past month. "How you put up with me, I'll never know."

The boat bobbed. The gulls circled. Annie watched the triangle of a sail float between them and shore.

"Maybe we shouldn't go any farther with this," she said, not at all sure that was what she wanted. She *didn't* want him humiliated.

"I thought you wanted me to do everything I used to."

"And how often did you used to?" Annie joked.

Luckily he took it as one. "You caught Dave's reference to the Party Barge, eh?"

"Is that what this was used for?"

"If you only knew." Knew he'd been damn near celibate for the past three years, for starters. He thought he'd have all the time in the world for the right woman to come along. And what if she had, at precisely the wrong time?

He found Annie with an outstretched arm and tugged her toward him. He stroked her cheek, his head tilted as he listened. "Tell me what you look like?"

"Again?"

"All I've got is your hair." He ran his hand across it, found a comb and touched it with his fingertips. "I want the shape of your face. Your eyes. Your skin."

Annie braced herself for another onslaught of sensation. Knowing that his senses were so acute made her keenly aware of every part he touched.

He outlined her face with both palms, measuring her cheekbones with his hands, her lips with his fingers, her nose, short and straight. The texture of her skin. Curved brows.

"Smile," he commanded softly, and felt her cheeks lift, the lines beside her eyes, the wide mouth. Her chin was round, her jaw subtle, her throat smooth. As were her shoulders, the warm skin at the base of her neck.

He didn't know the smile was gone, replaced by doubt. "You feel beautiful."

"I'm not."

"Says who?"

"You are," she said, changing the subject. "Beautiful, I mean."

He shook his head.

"Handsome then. You work at it." She couldn't prevent her hands from outlining the muscles on his arms. "It shows."

"Is that a compliment or a judgment?" Hands resting on her shoulders, he felt her shrug.

"A man who's careful of his appearance wants a woman with similar interests. I've never been that concerned with looks."

"It's what's inside that counts, right?"

"Yes. Not everyone thinks that."

"If I'm good-looking, I must be as shallow as your ex. Is that it?"

Annie pursed her lips for a minute, then looked back up at him. All she saw was her reflection. "This is where I'm supposed to say touché, right? It's a kind of pride, Cliff, wanting to be the best you can. But it's not a perfect world."

"And I have to accept me as I am."

"You want to be perfect."

"Not perfect, just me again. I know you've seen the bad side. There is another side of me. I wish I could show you."

Running his hand slowly down her body and back, he showed her a world of sensual intent. "Can't you feel what that does to me?" His hand closed on the outside of her thigh, his thumb tracing the high-cut leg of the bikini from the outside in, finding the narrow triangle of fabric, the curled hair.

Annie gasped. "Please."

Once again he was left guessing. "What does that mean?"

"It means I'm not ready for this. Neither of us are."

A flash of doubt, maybe anger, moved across his face like a fast-moving cloud over the sun. He didn't know, couldn't see what she wanted. She let him get close, then— Words weren't enough. What he needed was a good cold shower. "Do you think there are rocks in this water?"

It took her a moment to realize he was speaking literally. "Out here? Maybe thirty feet down."

"Good."

Cliff reached up and removed his glasses, calmly setting them on the seat. Then he placed one foot on the side of the boat, and in an arcing move, dived over.

"Cliff!" Annie screamed but couldn't stop him. He came up fifteen feet away, shaking the water out of his hair and keeping his eyes clamped shut. "What are you doing? Get back here!"

"I need the exercise!" he shouted. "And to tell you the truth, I need the cold water! Stay there."

She had no intention of moving. "Cliff," she said reprovingly, "nobody warned me you were self-destructive."

"I'm an excellent swimmer. There are no rocks, no sharks, and no boats for miles. I plan to work like hell for the next fifteen minutes. If I get too far, yell. Like you did just now," he murmured, smiling faintly. She might not want him, but she wasn't too keen on losing him, either.

Then he was off, doing a butterfly stroke that was exhausting to watch. Annie counted off the minutes on the dashboard clock, keeping one eye on the orange life jackets stuffed beside the engine compartment and one on Cliff's back, diving in the bright blue water.

She wanted to toss one of those life jackets at his head. "If he doesn't drown, I'm going to kill him," she muttered to herself.

By the time he'd followed her voice back and was grasping the ladder, Annie had reconsidered. He was obviously an accomplished swimmer, and the reasons he'd given her were sound and well thought out. About the only thing she could fault him for was the old wives' tale about not swimming after eating.

"A towel and a beer," she said, handing him one, then the other.

"Glasses, please?"

She handed him those and tried not to watch the water droplets glistening on his body as he perched on the edge of the boat in his clinging cutoffs. That spurt of exercise should have cooled them both off.

Cliff was grinning and breathing hard. "I didn't drown, did I?"

If he thought she was going to stand there and swallow his "I told you so," he could think again. With a cocky strut, she headed toward the front of the boat. "I've been telling you for three weeks you could do anything you used to."

Cliff lowered the beer in midgulp.

"Want to get this bucket started again, Captain? I've got packing to do for tomorrow's fair."

He headed toward the front, neatly sidestepping the cooler. "Keys in it?" he asked.

"Ready when you are."

From the sound of her voice he knew she was facing away. Figuring the width of the boat, and the length of the towel, Cliff wound it up, took aim and snapped his wrist.

Annie shrieked.

Cliff chuckled, imagining the part of her anatomy she was clutching. For once he'd gotten in the last word, not counting the unladylike expletive Annie tossed his way.

"Do you want to sell this?" As they crouched on either side of a packing crate, Annie held out one of the pots

Cliff had made. Another week had passed. He was helping her get ready for the first September art fair.

"Are you kidding? Sell *my* stuff? That's misrepresen-
tation. It's your booth."

"This has your name on it. You marked it here."

"Defaced it, you mean. It's just a pot."

"I like it. It's sturdy, masculine. The whorling on the
sides has your touch."

He reached out and she placed the bowl in his hand.
Their fingers met and skimmed briefly, then his hand
curled over hers, trapping it against the rim.

"You're flirting again," she said in a breathier voice
than she would have liked.

"No, I'm not." They'd agreed, silently perhaps, to
keep their distance. They were too naked, too needy, too
vulnerable, each in his own way, to get into a deeper relationship. It was true on the boat; it was true now.

Annie tried to bring them back to pottery. It was concrete, three-dimensional, easily set aside. "I'd buy your
work. It has style."

He broke into a grin that sent her pulse scurrying for
cover. His fingers followed that pulse up her wrist.

"Are you saying I have a distinctive touch?"

There was no point denying the effect he had on her.
Through sense and touch, he saw through her defenses.
"Cliff, I thought we agreed—"

"We did?" He ignored her words, concentrating on
that elusive beat beneath the flesh of her arm. Soft and
pale—at least that was how it felt. How would it taste?
Would her thighs match it for softness?

Annie jerked her hand away and the bowl crashed to
the floor. Cliff only smiled. "A priceless work of art ruined. What a shame."

"I'm sorry. That was really stupid. Let me get the broom."

He stopped her by touching her arm. "You ought to pay me for that."

"How?" His grin was easily interpreted. "On second thought, don't answer."

"You won't even guess?"

"Look, can we not crouch next to this crate like this? My thighs are killing me."

"You don't know what they're doing to me." His hand ran down the cotton of her slacks, taut over her flesh, warm toward the inside. She closed her legs but that only trapped him there. They sprang apart; he took it as a license to go farther.

Her voice was a soft threat in the dimness surrounding him, breathy, intense. "Don't."

"Why not?"

"I'll say yes." Her admission shocked them both. They'd reached a turning point neither was prepared for. "But if you reject me one more time, Cliff Sullivan, I swear..."

"I seem to be in the uncomfortable position of put up or shut up."

She sighed. "I didn't mean it that way."

"Close enough."

Cliff sat back on the concrete floor of the studio and ruffled his beard. Blind, sighted, what the hell difference did it make? But when it came right down to doing something about it, he wasn't ready.

That didn't mean he didn't ache for it.

"You're not the only one with doubts, you know," Annie said.

"Don't make up any on my account."

"I wonder sometimes whether you'd want me if you could see, or will when you can again."

"What do you think I'm waiting for? I don't relish making a fool of myself chasing after you when I can't do anything about it."

Annie spoke carefully, subduing her optimism about his operation with the caution her heart required. "You can't predict how you'll feel then. We should wait and—"

"And see. Ha."

They returned to packing the pottery in excelsior, Cliff ruefully congratulating himself on the growing acuteness of his hearing. He was getting good with voices. Like Dave's when his brother humored him. Or Annie's when she sensed he needed encouragement, or a hard-nosed knock at self-pity. And yet he wasn't really sure how she felt about him. If anything did develop between them, he had to be. He couldn't guess about something this important.

"That's the last crate." Annie slipped her hands into the loose pockets of her cotton slacks and played with her car keys. There was one more step Cliff needed to take, perhaps the biggest of all. "Why don't you come along?"

Cliff stopped scratching his beard. "To the art fair? And do what, look at the paintings?"

She wasn't sure she was helping or hindering him in the personal relations department, but at least he could joke about his handicap now.

"I admit it won't be a thrilling afternoon. I let the customers look without hassling them. But it'd be nice to have someone else along."

He took his time answering. Doubt from Cliff was rare. He was more likely to give her a flat no. "You wouldn't want me there."

"I asked, didn't I?"

"And this mountain man look? I haven't shaved in over four weeks. My hair's getting downright shaggy. I look like a throwback to the sixties."

"So do half the people at art fairs." That elicited a chuckle from him. "If you don't like the beard, shave it off."

"And cut my throat?"

"There are electric razors."

"Not to handle this forest. It'd have to be trimmed first."

"We'll stop at a barbershop on the way."

Cliff considered. Maybe the drive to the fair would be the perfect chance to talk to Annie, really talk.

On second thought, he should have cut his throat.

They drove in silence up I-75, an hour passing before they could mention the fiasco at the barbershop.

"Are you going to say anything?" Annie's voice was as tight as her hands on the steering wheel, or the outline of Cliff's jaw.

Even beneath the beard.

"So the barbershop didn't work out," she continued heatedly. "So yell. Blame me, blame him, just don't sit there like a mummy!"

Cliff replied with a unique, very foul expletive, then turned to look stonily out the window. Seeing nothing, he pictured it all. The barbershop, the mirrors, people sitting and waiting. And watching. Him being led in by Annie. He hated being led, so he took her hand as they came through the door. The curious would see no more than a couple holding hands.

They sat. He didn't look at the magazines, didn't check the end of season box scores in yesterday's paper. He listened to the humming razors and the ball game on what sounded like a radio old enough to have tubes. Cliff responded when the barber said "Sir" for the fourth time.

Or rather, Annie did. "Honey?" She leaned over and nuzzled his ear. "Forty-five-degree angle to your left, six paces." The woman was marvelous.

Cliff walked tall, knowing the barber would have the chair facing him. That's when he bumped into the part he forgot. The footrest. Smacking it with his shin, he tripped and grabbed the armrest for support. With all his weight unexpectedly thrown forward, the chair spun.

"Excuse me, sir," the solicitous older man said. "Are you all right?"

"Sorry." Cliff rubbed his shin and tried to get into the chair. He had the armrest firmly in his grip now. Problem was, it was the wrong armrest. His butt almost ended up in the hair clippings.

"Is he all right?" the barber had asked.

"Yes," Annie said, rushing over. Letting Cliff break a leg for the sake of pretending was pointless. "He's blind."

"Oh."

Cliff felt all eyes on him. How many? How many voices had he counted in the room before he'd gone into this slapstick routine? How many mirrors replaying it from how many angles?

"Come on!" He grabbed Annie's arm and headed out. This time he was leading. Somehow they made it to the street. "Where's the goddamn truck?"

Riding in silence now, having earned no replies to her outburst, Annie had had enough. "I'm a teacher," she began quietly, getting a better grip on the wheel, "not a miracle worker. If you would learn to take things a little slower, to ask for help, to walk slower instead of full speed ahead as if nothing's wrong..."

She hit the turn signal and it ticked steadily. The engine whined as she downshifted on the exit ramp. "Cliff, I'm sorry about what happened. But I am not going to handle all this guilt on my own."

"Guilt?" He blew. Annie was ready for it. "Why should you feel guilty?"

"Because I dragged you into something you weren't ready for."

"I've been going to barbers since my first haircut. Don't give me that—" He let loose with another series of curses to describe exactly what he thought of her analysis. "I should have known there'd be a footrest."

"Don't blame it on yourself."

"Look, my life is not your fault!"

"Agreed!"

"All right!"

"We're here!"

"Good!"

"Now can we stop screaming at each other like some kind of married couple?"

Annie parked and jumped out. This was as ridiculous as the disaster at the barbershop. Of course it was her fault. She'd gotten him in too deep too fast. She knew Cliff wouldn't slow down; she had to pace things for him. She'd have to find another way to counteract this setback.

Maybe her best alternative was right before her. "Will you help me set up for the fair, please?"

Cliff clenched and unclenched his fist. He couldn't very well sit here and sulk, like Kane, who had been left behind. His shin throbbed, sunlight streamed through the windshield, and the draft of air coming in her opened door was brisk and smelled of cider and the first sharp days of autumn. Maybe he could show her he wasn't totally helpless. God knows, he needed a dose of confidence right now. "What do I do?"

Annie breathed a sigh of relief. "That's what we're going to find out."

The fair went as smoothly as the barbershop had gone badly. The awning went up without a hitch. Annie held her breath every time Cliff insisted on pounding in the stakes, but he managed. The shelves were readily assembled on tables provided by the local Lions Club. Annie and Cliff covered them with cloth, unpacked her wares and sat back in mismatched director's chairs.

Making conversation, Annie shared the lowdown on the local art world. Chimes tinkled along the edges of their awning.

"Excuse me," a woman interrupted. "I have a niece in Tennessee. Would it be safe to ship her these? They'd make a lovely wedding gift."

"Thank you," Annie replied, rising. "Cliff, would you please get me one of the smaller crates while I write this up?"

"Sure."

He ventured two strides behind the awning, felt among the crates and gingerly stepped back inside. Annie kept the conversation going so he'd know where both women stood. He handed her a crate and sat down.

So the day went. Errand boy. Trained but not very useful. Questions directed at him by customers were deflected, "Sorry, she's the artist." He was feeling good and sorry for himself and he knew it.

Racking her brain for things he could help with, Annie kept an eye on the lines furrowing his forehead. That's when she noticed the woman coming around the back of the awning toward him. Fortyish, well groomed, impeccably blond.

"Excuse me," the woman said.

Cliff barely turned his head. It sounded to him as if Annie would be busy for the rest of the day.

The woman touched his arm. He jumped.

Her tinkling laughter sounded through the awning, leaving Annie hard-pressed to explain what was so immediately irritating about it.

"I'm so sorry," the woman said to Cliff in a honeyed voice. "You were lost in thought."

"I'm sorry myself," he said, nodding politely.

Annie itched to get over there, but she was quoting prices to a local couple and customers were browsing three deep at the other table. Even out of the corner of her eye she couldn't miss the blatant way the woman raked Cliff's body with her eyes. Small consolation to Annie that he didn't catch it.

"I was wondering if you could show me some of your bigger pieces," the woman said.

"I'll bet," Annie muttered under her breath. Blind or not, this woman was sending out signals a two-by-four would pick up.

Cliff showed her to the first display table, turning on that slow smile of his. Annie's blood became a curdled stream.

Exclaiming over every piece Cliff touched, Blondie put her hand on his arm and wrapped herself around it like a vine.

Completing a sale, Annie pulled the charge plate handle across the card so hard that it grated. She snapped it back with a satisfying thwack.

"Oh, I *love* that." The woman ran her hands over a pot. "I've watched potters at work, you know, the way they use their hands. Will you be having a demonstration today?''

"Not today," Cliff replied.

Annie's mouth dropped open.

"I do think it's one of the more sensual arts, don't you?"

Cliff scratched his beard. "Now that you mention it, I've been told I have a good touch."

The woman grinned like a barracuda. "I hope you don't mind my getting personal, but I've always loved men in beards."

Probably always loved men in pants, Annie thought blackly.

That's when Cliff rubbed his knuckles against his beard and ducked his head in a patented James Dean move.

That bastard! He'd used that move on her. What was worse, it had worked then, too. If Annie hadn't been holding up a four-gallon urn to show the price tag, she'd have thrown it at Cliff Sullivan's head.

"What would you suggest?" the woman asked, eyeing the pieces once more. "It's for my bedroom."

"Of course it is," Annie practically shouted, but the cozy couple was too engrossed to notice.

"How about this?" Cliff asked.

Oh, no. Annie held her breath. He'd accidentally picked up the same pot he'd put down moments before.

"Aha!" The woman's laugh was tinkling and false. "Artistic and humorous, too. What other qualities does the man possess?"

"I can think of one that would surprise you," Annie remarked, coming up beside them.

Squeezing between the two to set the pot back down, she wasn't above physically disengaging Blondie's hand from Cliff's arm. Better than breaking it off at the wrist, she reasoned. "I'm Annie Rosetti and this is my work." She might as well have said "my man." "I'd be happy to show you anything *else* you're interested in."

"That's quite all right," the woman responded frostily. "I like to discover them on my own."

Cliff smiled and nodded, seeing nothing. That he'd missed Blondie's meaningful look as she departed was the only thing that gave Annie any satisfaction. As her next four customers came and went, she was fuming like a chimney stack.

"I suppose you thought that was funny," she said.

Cliff put his arm out like a railroad crossing barrier to stop her charging past. She'd been avoiding him while sending out sparks for the past fifteen minutes.

She batted his hand down. "You enjoy misleading women?"

"Are we talking about her or you?"

Annie shot him a look, then ground her teeth at the uselessness of it. "She thought you could see."

"Harmless fun," he said, shrugging.

"Harmless?"

"Why shouldn't I respond to a woman who admires me? All's fair—"

"In love. This was just . . . just lust!"

"Were you worried I'd actually go off with her?"

"She doesn't even know you."

"Doesn't know about my eyes you mean."

"You! Anything about you!"

"The woman I want keeps turning me down."

Annie crossed her arms. "And so she should if you treat her like this."

"Like what? Ever since the boat you've been keeping away from me. You never let me touch you!"

"Shh. There are people around." In fact, two of them turned their heads as they passed the little argument in stall 51.

Explaining as tersely as he could, Cliff said, "I can't sit here and do nothing. I was feeling useless."

Annie heard only the excuses he was making. He was everything she'd taught herself to avoid. Gorgeous, vain; if a woman pawed and babied and praised him enough, he'd respond. Just like Ken. "Let's just stick to business for the rest of the day. Can you do that?"

"Please, I need to drive."

His arm was stretched across the back seat and he was playing with her hair. Again. His fingertips managed to brush her neck just often enough to make the hairs rise.

"I need to know where I stand with you, Annie."

"Out in left field, or haven't you figured that out?"

She was still fuming. He'd given her enough time to simmer down. "I'm tired of playing student. I want more."

"From anyone who will give it to you?"

Her head was pounding from hours of wanting to scream instead of smiling and waiting on people. Never had she wanted more to be alone.

In wrinkled cotton slacks and a silk T-shirt, she didn't feel the least bit sexy right now, no matter how his fingers strummed those traitorous raised hairs. If he had seen her these past few weeks in her Indian cottons and loose men's shirts, smocks and coveralls spattered with clay, he'd know she couldn't possibly compete with that woman at the fair. *Any* of those women, pushing baby strollers, holding hands with their husbands, picking out wedding gifts.

Cliff hadn't been able to compare. Someday he would.

"We've got to talk."

"We've got to talk," Cliff agreed.

Annie sighed. "We really do. About us. This can't go on the way it has."

"Hear, hear." He traced the shell of her ear until she thought she'd scream or run off the road.

"Annie?"

"What?"

"We have to talk about when we're going to make love."

Six

―

Annie ground the gears as she downshifted. The screech could have been her nerves. "Don't start."

"Give me one good reason."

"There's no future in it."

He sat back stiffly. He hadn't expected her to be quite so blunt. "You don't think the operation will work?"

"I do. That's why I'm being honest. You'll see I'm not your type. Take my word for it." It tore her a little inside, like a seam coming apart, but it was better to say it now. All her daydreams about their going to art fairs together, talking, joking and sharing, would never come true.

"You think I'm looking for a 'type'?"

"You're good-looking," she hedged. "Women flock to you."

"Not lately." He meant the past three years.

Annie thought of the past few weeks. "Thanks a lot."

"I didn't mean it that way. You're different." No woman had gotten as close to him as she had. At times it was nearly impossible not to blurt out his frustrations. But he wouldn't burden her with that. He'd already put her through dark moods, bad days, outbursts of temper. She'd stuck by him through all of it. Was she turning him away now?

He listened to her silence and the hum of the tires. They were slowing down. He caught the difference between her short asphalt drive and his gravel one.

"We're here," she said.

His place.

"This is your idea of talking?"

"Cliff, I don't know what you mean when you say I'm different. It's you who's changed, and that's only temporary. When your eyes heal, you'll go back to the mines and the Upper Peninsula. Maybe the women, too."

The sound of crickets and waves rose around them when she cut the engine.

He cursed softly. "I know you have this idea I'm some kind of wolf. It's half my fault. I wanted you to see me as I was, no, *better* than I was. I wanted you to want me."

"I did."

He tried to detect false sincerity, but Annie was never false. Her admission hung in the air. "Then why won't you let me near you?"

She touched his lips with her fingertips. It was late, dark. Without the instrument lights she could barely make out his profile. "I want you too much. That's what I'm afraid of. That I won't want to let go."

"You think you're the only one who's afraid?"

Sitting here talking quietly, Annie knew she'd wanted this with him, the intimacy, the honesty. Aching for him to reach out in some way, not as a student but as a man.

But she'd seen his barriers come and go before. How long would the closeness last?

For now she didn't care. She'd take it as it came. She touched her lips to his and felt his arms going around her waist, pulling her across the seat to him.

She was trembling. That was fine with him. Damn fine, in fact. When he leaned back, she stretched a little farther, her breasts pressed against his chest. She steadied herself by bracing her hand against his thigh. That was fine with him, too.

He tore his mouth from hers. One more thing needed to be said. "I was an insecure jerk today. I don't usually go after women like that. I mean it. Apology accepted?"

"Mmm-hmm." It was all she could answer with him nibbling her lip. She wondered if they'd steam up the windows. The way he was playing with the inside of her elbow made her whole arm shimmy. When he rasped the silk of her T-shirt against the nub of her breast, the arm gave way.

"Ever made love in the front seat of a truck?" he whispered.

Body to body, his mouth against her ear, Annie was having trouble formulating a sentence. Dimly she knew her answer was no. Either way it was only a matter of minutes before that changed to yes. Whatever her doubts had been, they were lost in the swirl of his thumb teasing her collarbone, the silk of her shirt, the satiny underside of his tongue.

A brilliant yellow light pierced her eyes.

"Oh, it's you," Dave called from the porch, briefly blocking the light with his body as he sauntered toward them.

Annie scrambled upright, knocking her knee against the stick shift on the floor.

"So he *is* here," Dave said, grinning. He directed an explanation toward his brother. "Heard the truck and thought maybe you were out here fumbling around in the dark."

"Hardly," Cliff growled. With Annie off him, he pulled himself into a sitting position and got out of the truck. "Point me in the right direction," he muttered. "I'll strangle him."

"Uh, see you later," Dave said, waving as he backed up slowly. "Hey, here's someone who wants to see you!" With that he let the dog out of the house and ducked inside. "Night, Annie!"

In two bounding leaps Kane heaved himself onto Cliff, yipping excitedly enough to send the chipmunks scurrying into their burrows for a hundred yards around.

"Down, damn it!" He might just as well command his body to do the same, Cliff thought grimly, grabbing the dog by the collar and following the woodslat walkway to the pen.

"You keep him out all night?" Annie asked, strolling behind at an amused distance.

Cliff found the chain and hooked Kane up. "Can't keep him in on a night like this."

It *was* a beautiful night, Annie realized. The slosh of tiny stones being washed in the waves, the warm and humid Indian summer breeze rolling in over the water. There was a nip in the air—just enough to spell night.

"I'm here," she said, holding out her hand.

Cliff found it, and they stood side by side as Kane whimpered and panted from his pen.

"There's a moon, almost full. I can see it reflected in your glasses." Annie talked softly. She liked the night, and someone to share it with. "The stars are out. The porch light is on."

"My soon-to-be-ex-brother's addition to the house."

"No-o-o," she chided. "Maybe he thought you were being attacked by a temporarily insane woman in the cab of her truck."

"He's going back to school next week."

"Is he?"

In the quiet and dark, with only their hands touching, their thoughts followed the same path. It was Cliff who spoke. "We won't be interrupted again, Annie."

She suddenly felt hollow, like a vase or a just-fired urn. Some things stood alone; some were only waiting to be filled.

"Cliff," she began, although she had no idea what she wanted or how to say it.

Cliff knew exactly what he wanted, and it sure as hell wasn't temporary. In fact, this first step would take some planning on his part. He released her hand and headed up the path. "Will you come by tomorrow?"

Although her courage had deserted her, Annie found her voice as she stood rooted at the end of the path. It was a night for truth. "I—I wasn't planning on it. I believe our lessons are finished."

There it was. She'd taught him what she could, and in the process had gone way beyond lessons. Her surge of jealousy this afternoon only proved what she'd been feeling for weeks. She loved him. If he didn't return those feelings, better to set him free now.

"School's out," she said lightly, knowing his hearing was keen and her heart heavy. "You've learned everything I can teach you."

Not everything, Cliff thought, not by a long shot. Lessons had never been what he was after. At first he'd wanted a woman to convince him he was still a man. Petty, maybe, but he'd needed that and he'd gone after it. In return, what she'd taught him ran deeper than can openers or clay pots. He heard it every time she spoke; she accepted him as he was—she might even love him. She just wasn't admitting it yet.

Uh-uh, Annie Rosetti, you're wrong about school. The lesson plans he had in mind involved feelings, not pottery. Perhaps he'd start with a session on trust. After his blundering today, they could both use that. And some one-on-one tutorials regarding men, women and their ancient but thoroughly modern modes of interaction. He could think of half a dozen modes right now.

What had she said that first day of class? *Anything you create will be beautiful.* They had thousands of memories to create. And tomorrow wasn't too soon to start.

"I've learned all about your house," Cliff said casually, hands in pockets. "What about my dryer, my dishwasher? All the appliances are different here. How will I run them when Dave's gone?"

Annie stood openmouthed. She felt as if she'd just been slapped by a particularly cold wave. *Was that all he wanted her for? Lessons?* Okay, maybe she'd asked for this by insisting on the teacher and pupil arrangement until the bitter end, but up until a moment ago she could have sworn he felt differently.

Just shows you what a woman can fall for when she thinks with her hormones instead of her brain. "Classes," she said flatly.

Cliff heard the tension in her voice from the back porch. He fought a grin and lost. "Eight in the morning sound okay, teach?"

"What happened to ten o'clock?"

Her voice got sharp when she was peeved. Very sharp.

"I'll make breakfast," he offered, rocking back on his heels and jingling some spare change. "Under your supervision, of course."

"Of course," Annie ground out. So he wanted his free lessons to continue. No more talk of making love, not even a good-night kiss. She'd remember that in the morning.

"Morning, teach." Cliff smiled and slid the beachside door open.

She'd come over feeling decidedly snappish. One look at Cliff and her heart lurched. He was wearing a cutoff T-shirt that emphasized the ripples of his abdomen, cutoff jeans and those ratty Topsiders. She wanted to ask him if that was all he ever wore but decided it'd be safer not to call attention to it. He smelled like soap and looked like he'd gotten out of the shower not long before. His hair was getting so long that Annie suspected it would still be damp. Of course, the only way to test that theory would be to run her hands through it.

She buried her fists in the pockets of her peasant skirt and stepped through the door, using her knees to prevent Kane from squeezing out. "Hi, beast."

The door closed with an airtight whoosh. Annie smelled after-shave. The man didn't shave. That meant he'd dabbed on cologne. For her sake. Under the anger, something began to tingle.

Vigorously she cleared her throat. "Where's Dave?"

"You're not going to ask what that wonderful aroma is?"

She'd already speculated on the wonderful aroma.

"I've got sausage in the skillet and omelet-makings ready to go. We were just waiting for you."

"Smells great." If that was sausage, it was the only kind in existence that smelled like musky male cologne.

She followed him into the kitchen, plastering a smile on her face as they rounded the doorway. The table was empty.

Two place settings.

No Dave.

"I thought you said '*we* were waiting'?"

Kane trotted into the room on cue. "Sure," Cliff said, scratching the dog's ears.

Annie scraped out the nearest chair and plopped down. "How about if I watch my star pupil make breakfast?" The sensation of being out maneuvered finally hit home. No doubt he'd be as competent in his own kitchen as he was in hers. So why the invitation? Her nerve endings went on red alert.

"Anything you say, teach." Cliff patted the counter for the tub of butter, wondering how he knew through sense alone that she was sitting there with her lips pursed, arms folded and legs crossed. Maybe tension communicated itself in waves of some kind.

A pat of melting butter hissed in the pan. Cliff poured in the eggs. "Aren't you curious about the makings of a legendary Sullivan Omelet?"

Annie squared her shoulders and decided she was being silly. She was a grown woman, free to call the shots here, free to say no to anything she felt was getting out of hand. Although, judging from the way her nerves sizzled, if he touched her she might melt like that pat of butter.

She clutched the countertop, a good three feet from him. "Secret ingredients?"

"Old family recipe." He pulled a short knife out of the silverware drawer and proceeded to dice a green pepper.

Watching the deftness with which he handled the knife, Annie held her breath.

"Voilà!" he said, scooping a handful off the cutting board.

Annie's breath came out in a rush.

"Wait'll you see me flip these omelets."

"Wait'll you see me scrape them off the floor!"

At that he laughed. So did she. The tension eased out of her like that rush of breath. She *liked* him. If she could keep her hormones in check, they might even come out of this friends. "You've been practicing."

"Always known how. Meet Cliff Sullivan, Bachelor Chef."

And perfect host, Annie admitted. She ceased hovering and let him finish preparing the meal while she set out plates and poured coffee. By the time they were through eating, Annie was scolding herself for being so untrusting. He'd shown her another side of himself, not glowering but not wolfish, either.

"My compliments to the chef."

"*Merci.*"

She patted her stomach. "I could get used to eating breakfasts like that."

"Most important meal of the day. Better when you have someone to share it with, though."

How right he was, she thought wistfully. That could apply to a lot of things. "Cliff..."

He hopped up. "You wash, I'll dry?"

She swallowed her argument for now, almost relieved. Just his being near made her emotions a muddle. "I thought you had a dishwasher."

"Okay then. You rinse, I'll load."

Five minutes later Cliff excused himself. Soft music wafted in from the living room. Soothing. Romantic. Not rock and roll. If she wanted coffee, she'd have to join him in there. Too late, she remembered the red alert.

"Exactly where is Dave?" She was antsy and ready to get to work. Sitting beside him in this intimate setting, even at nine in the morning, was asking for trouble.

But he remained resolutely sociable. With one foot on the coffee table, he unself-consciously slouched back to scratch Kane's ears.

Annie noticed the washboard effect of his abdomen between the cropped T-shirt and the shorts. She suspected it was there to be noticed.

"Dave got himself a part-time job down at the marina," Cliff said, making conversation. "'Tis the season for taking boats out of the water. Said you were keeping me so busy, he had to find some way to entertain himself."

"Oh?"

"Some*one*, I bet. There's no end of pretty girls down there."

"Is that where your reputation got started?"

He gritted his teeth and let the emotion slide. He had a lot of bridge building to do.

"Dave thinks you're a regular Don Juan."

"Dave's got an outdated opinion of me." And so do you, Cliff thought, his face dark. "It applied in college. I've grown some since then."

"I know you have." Annie sighed apologetically. An accident like the one he'd been through would change anyone. But would he go back to his old ways when the blindness was cured?

Cliff was quiet, the music soothing, the couch fluffy and soft. Annie rearranged her big skirt so that she could curl her legs under her.

Cliff reached out quickly. "Where are you going?"

His nervousness caught her by surprise. She wasn't the only one waiting for something to happen. "Just getting situated," she said. If he wasn't ready for a lesson, perhaps talking would ease things. If sharing and closeness were what she wanted, maybe it was time she asked for it. "Will you tell me about the explosion?"

Cliff thought a moment. "You, a handful of inspectors from the Bureau of Mines, OSHA, the Department of Alcohol, Tobacco and Firearms. Who else wants to know?"

"Tobacco and Firearms?"

"They regulate blasting, along with half a dozen government agencies. Accidents like this aren't supposed to happen. Faulty blasting cap, they think. They ran me and the company through a—a cartload of questions before they came to that conclusion. Was I on drugs? Was the mine operating under unsafe working conditions? Were the blasting caps stored improperly?"

"None of which was true?"

"Not a'tall, lassie, not a'tall."

"Ah." She watched him absentmindedly scratch his beard.

"Luckily no one else was hurt," he said. "All I remember is grabbing my eyes. Hurt like hell. Worst part was not knowing how bad it would be. When they told me about cornea transplants, it was like a reprieve from death row."

Annie squeezed his hand. "I can imagine."

His mouth was grim, caught up in his memories, but his hand on hers was getting warm. When their fingers entwined, she knew she shouldn't have touched him. She wanted to be his lover; she just didn't think she could stand him changing his mind afterward.

"Maybe we should wait until you see me, get your job back, get back to your regular life...."

"Maybe we should," he responded. She was still hesitating. Maybe she was right. He cared too much about her to tie her down to his disability. When he was better—hell, when he was himself again he could imagine how great it would be for them. He was better than this, smarter, quicker, less clumsy. That was what he wanted most of all, for the real Cliff Sullivan to meet the real Annie Rosetti.

"Maybe you could do me a favor," he said, disengaging his hand. "Get me the scissors, please?"

"Scissors?"

He rubbed his beard as if it were hairy sandpaper. "I want you to trim this damn thing so I can cut it."

Annie rolled her eyes. Caught off balance again. "Where are they?"

For the next ten minutes they were busy. Annie filled a bowl with steaming water, found towels, lather and soap, while Cliff fetched the razor off the bathroom sink.

Spreading newspapers beneath a kitchen chair, Annie announced they were ready. Cliff sat. She glanced at his thighs, muscular and large, at the way the cutoff T-shirt ended so far short of his belt loops. She hadn't been so close to him all morning. She snapped open a towel and wrapped it around his shoulders. "Okay, Samson, here we go."

"Not the hair."

"I can't do the hair."

"Just the beard."

"Just the beard."

The music softly surrounded them, along with the snip-snip of scissors. With one hand Annie bent the hair of his beard back so that it would stand out from his skin.

With her other hand she carefully trimmed it down to a prickly stubble. Before long she was engrossed in the feel of it against her fingers—bouncy, stiff, springy.

Her breath fell lightly on the side of his neck just below his ear. Cliff turned.

"Don't. I'll poke you."

"Sorry."

She worked around his ear. Glancing up, she realized she could see behind his glasses. He had smile lines; she'd noticed, but not how deeply etched. She'd never seen the dark lashes resting on his cheeks when his eyes were closed. They opened. She saw the milkiness, immediately overcome with guilt. It was something she knew he wouldn't want her to see.

"How much of these sideburns do you want to lose?" she asked.

"An inch maybe. Here." He indicated a spot with his finger, hoping he could keep it steady.

Maybe this wasn't such a good idea. He'd planned a quiet morning alone, without games, to show her he was trustworthy, that he was more than a Lothario. That was lesson number one. He hadn't planned on her driving him wild with her touch. Sometimes her blouse or her breasts brushed his arm. When she worked her way around the front, he spread his knees and she hesitantly stepped inside.

He crumpled a towel across his lap, trying to think calming thoughts, but her hands kept doing those impossibly erotic things to his beard, and her breath kept winnowing through his hair like wind through a field.

His shaving brush clacked against its ceramic cup as Annie whipped up the lather. "Ready?"

"As I'll ever be," he answered, mouth dry.

Annie knocked the lather off the brush. Shave and a haircut, two bits. Chuckling, she smoothed it on, dabbing his nose with a towel when she put a dollop there by mistake. "Now where's the razor?"

"Here." He put his hand on a flat leather box.

"You can't be serious!" Annie stared at the silver straight razor gleaming against velvet. "You could kill people with this thing."

"Now you know what I mean about cutting my throat. An electric razor would choke on a beard this thick."

"But I don't know how..."

"I trust you." He leaned his head back and bared his throat. Lesson number two.

Annie swallowed. He couldn't be this relaxed. After touching him, smelling him, feeling the warmth and power of his body for the past fifteen minutes, she was almost shaking. Her hands certainly were. "You're either brave, crazy or both."

"You work with your hands," he said confidently.

"Clay doesn't bleed."

She put one finger under his chin and got in position to scrape. That meant standing behind him, his head cushioned against her breasts.

"Mmmm," he said.

"Don't grin. Don't move. Don't even breathe. If I cut your throat, I swear I'll kill you."

He chuckled, and she felt the cords in his throat rumble. This was sheer hell. A sneaky feeling of remorse said she owed him after suggesting they visit the barbershop yesterday. That didn't make it any easier. In fact, the physical risk made her all the more aware of his skin, his smell, the cologne intensified by the damp towel draped over his shoulders.

One scrape and Annie was back to business. Concentrating intensely, she came around the side. One hand held the razor at an angle, her arm circling the back of his head. The other hand tipped his chin. She wiped the razor, and silver gleamed. The smooth patches of skin grew larger. She touched them with her fingertip to stretch the skin for the next pass.

Then she reached the front and stepped between his legs. That should have been the easy part. He pulled down his upper lip, bit his lower lip and contorted his cheek to one side so that she could shave around his mouth.

The funny faces didn't register. All she felt was him reaching out to pull her closer. Her own cropped top left her midriff as bare as his. He found it.

A dollop of lather fell from the razor onto his jeans. Rushing to wipe it off, she touched the fullness behind his zipper. "Uh, sorry."

Suddenly the tension was as thick as the razor was thin and sharp.

"The music," she said, her voice husky, her throat tight, "It's stopped."

"Okay," was all he said, his hands falling to his thighs.

She walked over to the stereo and turned the record over with trembling hands. This just wouldn't do. Half his face was bare now; he was a man she wasn't sure she recognized. That should be a warning. He kept so much to himself. How much did she really know?

Unfortunately one thing was certain—she couldn't leave him half-shaved. Only two more passes along his right cheek and she'd be finished. "Ready?"

Can't you tell? he thought.

Annie stood on his left to reach around and shave the right side, tipping his head against her. Once again she was engrossed, her face inches from his hair. Yes, it was still damp.

Her breasts were warm, the silk of her shirt, well, silky. Cliff knew all he had to do was look up and he'd be inches from her lips— "Ouch."

She jumped. "You shouldn't have turned like that!"

"My fault. I know." He wiped his face clean with the towel.

Annie peered at the small cut. "Guess you'll live."

Cliff touched her cheek with his hand. It wasn't hard to find her lips from here. Full, moist and coffee-warmed. Her lips paused, then parted. His tongue probed, then he waited. When the kiss was over, she said nothing. "Aren't you going to argue?"

Again nothing. Her fingertips stroked his cheek. In a way the beard had softened him. Now the planes of his cheeks were sharper, indelibly defined. The lines around his mouth were clearer. She ran her hand up his cheek to his glasses.

"Leave them on," he said. He could only bare so much; he didn't want her seeing that.

She knew if she wanted him she'd have to accept him as he was—no promises, no excuses, some things kept to himself.

And let the hearts fall where they may. That's what love was. It wasn't conditional; it didn't wait for operations or guarantees. It was suddenly important that she let him know that.

She ran her hands over his face, unable to stop touching his skin, pink from the hot water. "There's something about kissing a man in sunglasses. It's very erotic."

He turned and kissed her palm. "It's sexy in the dark."

"Cliff."

"Shh. Let me kiss you, touch you. I can't gaze into your eyes. This is all I have." He found the opening under her blouse and ran his hands over her love-tight breasts. From there he wrapped his arms around her and coaxed her onto his lap. "Are you going to stop me, Annie?"

"Are you going to make love to me?"

"Yes."

"No."

Their mouths met, explored, luxuriated. It could have lasted for hours; Annie wouldn't have known. The only change was the progress of his hand tracing up her thigh. "I'm too heavy," she said, feeling self-conscious, feeling what this was doing to him.

"Let me say that," he mumbled against her neck. "When I'm on top."

The sound of her moan made him ache, especially when she pressed against his arousal. Her thigh became warm as his hand moved along it.

She shifted. His fingers found lace. "Panties?"

She nodded weakly as his finger outlined the opening. His hands were everywhere, and no matter how she ran hers through his hair or down his clean-shaven face, she couldn't stop thinking about them, feeling them through silk lace until it felt like he was seducing her soul.

The chair was hard and small. If he tipped her back any farther in his arms, they'd fall. There were things he wanted to do that couldn't be done sitting up. Like stretching her out and examining every recumbent inch.

Her lips were wet and hot against his, as moist as the lips his fingers parted under the damp silk between her legs.

She let out a muffled cry.

"Don't stop me now, Annie."

"No . . . I . . . maybe we should go upstairs."

Cliff tried to picture a bed, with Annie looking up at him. What if he fumbled, made mistakes? "We could turn off the lights."

"It's morning," she reminded him gently.

"Damn daylight saving time."

She chuckled, burningly aware of his fingers touching her, leaving a trail of honey down her thigh.

"I wanted to make love to you in the dark. We'd be equal then."

She wrapped her arms around his neck. He couldn't withdraw into his doubts now; she wouldn't let him. So much of his self-esteem depended on how he felt about her and them together. "I'll close my eyes," she whispered. "I just want to feel you. Inside."

Seven

___

He wanted her, but he was going to lead this time. They stood, Cliff reaching behind her knees. "I'm going to carry you to my cave, woman." He waited for her protest.

She nodded, letting her nose skim his cheek so that he sensed it. He needed to show her he could do this. Besides, she doubted her trembling legs would hold her up much longer.

He knew where the stairs were. A short command to Kane stopped the dog at the foot of them. Cliff found the loft, then the bed, and set Annie down. He found the skin at her waist, his thumbs hooking into the waistband of her skirt. "Is this a button?"

She touched his arm in an up-and-down motion and heard the button ping across the room.

Hands trembling, she lifted her blouse over her head. When he found her hands covering her breasts, he tilted his head quizzically.

"I feel so naked around you. You see so much with your hands. I don't know how to hide."

"Do you want to?"

"Not anymore."

He drew his own shirt over his head, flinging it where he'd probably never find it. He brought her hands to his sides, their bodies meeting above the waist, tingling and bare.

Cliff dipped his mouth to her collarbone, tracing the lightest of perfumes, catching the scented powder under her arms, heating to musk. Tangy, sweet. As sweet as her own mouth murmuring his name.

He slowly unfastened the button on his cutoffs, drawing down the zipper but leaving them on. First he had to pull her close, the small circling motion of his hips rubbing denim against silk panties. The sound made them both hot.

"That's hearing. What about taste, Annie? What do you want me to—"

She had only to open her mouth and he was there, sliding her back onto the bed, holding her head in place while he thrust with his tongue and she took.

She was wrong about his sensing everything. He couldn't see what was in her eyes. If he made a fool of himself, he'd never see the pity there. That made him all the more determined there would be none. Only desire, the way he showed her how to stroke him, and excitement in her small gasp when he licked, then bit. His whole body was pumped. The need to make love, now, overrode any anxiety.

He found her with his hand, and entered. "Lord, you feel good," he breathed. "Tight."

She murmured something nonverbal; it didn't matter. He heard her hair whispering against the pillow as her head swayed back and forth, sensations rocketing through her.

"Don't stop," she pleaded.

She must be looking at him, intense, imploring. Damn.

"What is it? Don't stop."

"I feel like I'm on a stage, performing for an audience who can see me, but I can't see them."

She stroked his hair.

He flinched. "Don't."

"Maybe I'm not exciting enough to keep your mind off your doubts."

"Exciting? Lady, you're what got me here in the first place. If I could give you back even half of what you've given me... You've stood by me. God knows I haven't earned it. I've given you one hard time after another."

"Love isn't a matter of earning. It's either given or it's not. If someone doesn't love you, it doesn't matter how many points you try to rack up. You'll never please them."

Cliff lay back on the bed, one arm thrown over his eyes, his body stretched and taut, his desire heavy.

Love. Is that what she'd been giving him all along? Probably, and he'd been too self-centered to realize it. But did he have the guts to return that kind of feeling? Especially in the condition he was in, this limbo between seeing and not seeing?

"What are you thinking?"

He didn't answer. He was thinking he wanted her to be in love, because that would make two of them.

"Mind if I just look?" she asked after a moment's quiet, resting her hand lightly on his chest.

He laughed, or rather smiled that primitively male smile. "At least I have a couple good points."

"Shall I count the ways? There's this," she said, stroking the ridge of his abdominal muscle. "This." She brushed the lateral muscle that ran from his back around to his hip.

He quivered at the lightly tickling touch.

"This," she continued, running her fingers up his thigh. "And this. Is this a muscle?"

Every muscle in his body was rigid by now, particularly the one she was touching.

He cleared his throat. Twice.

She touched her lips to his chest, one kiss for each nipple and one in between. "Your eyes have nothing to do with your being a man, Cliff. Not to me."

When he finally spoke, his voice was as tight as the self-control reining him in. "This I don't need to be taught, Annie."

"I wouldn't dream of it."

"What do you dream of?"

She touched his cheek. "Making love with you."

Cliff grabbed her arms, part anger, part naked need. "If that's the case, don't touch me with kid gloves anymore."

"All right." She kissed him then, hard, open, one leg across his. She had never done anything as wanton in her life; if Cliff minded, he didn't show it.

In fact, she was under him so fast it took her a moment to get her bearings. That fast he was on her, spreading her legs and uttering her name as if it were some dark magic spell. Then he was in her, a quick, blunt thrust.

Cliff caught his breath, startled by her cry. What the hell was he doing? "Are you all right?"

"I'm fine," she replied, stunned and breathless. "Please."

She rubbed her cheek on his like a cat, her body trembling like a woman. He groaned and slid in and out on honey. Long, slow. Her skin shimmered beneath his like a heat wave. And he heard his voice whispering words to which she responded, with motion and sound, unleashing something in him, something it took two to quench.

Their bodies were solid, matched, physical. His was heavy. The hair on his legs grazed hers until they wrapped around him. Running her foot down the back of his leg, she found a bony ankle. Even that was sensitive.

But nothing like the part of her he found with his thumb. "Do you like that?"

What a question, she thought, laughter rumbling up inside her.

Cliff gritted his teeth; he almost lost it right there. "Don't do that. It makes you quiver. Here." He put the flat of his hand on her abdomen, pressing softly. She moaned and clenched around him.

How masochistic could a man get? He was practically exploding. He tried to distract himself, to hold on.

"Right down here," he murmured, stroking her softly, listening to her pleasure. "Where babies come from."

He lifted himself off her slowly, completely. "I don't know if we can go any farther with this."

"What's wrong? What did you say?"

"We've got to think of what might happen."

"Let it." She couldn't keep the flash of anger out of her voice. Her skin was flushed, her body clamoring for release. But her heart, when he left her like this, was gallingly empty.

"I'm talking about birth control," he said. "We forgot that."

Annie flopped back on the bed. Cliff heard her soft curse. "You don't have any...?" she asked.

"They're hard enough to put on when I can see."

"Oh."

His jaw was tight, more obvious now with the shave, Annie noticed. She knew he was right. And thoughtful. And she'd almost gotten carried away into what, emotional risks aside, could have been a major mistake. "Do you like children?"

"I hadn't planned on having any quite so soon."

She chuckled and stopped abruptly. Even the memory of him inside her made her blood pound. "That's not what I was getting at."

"Making polite conversation?" He was the frustrated one now. Boy, he was blowing this. Why hadn't he thought ahead? "Maybe Dave has some in the medicine cabinet. He ought to. I've lectured him on it enough."

He got up and strode to the bathroom with that unhesitating walk. Annie lay back and simply admired the walk, the way his muscles moved. "Cute buns," she whispered to herself. She rested her cheek on her bent arm and laughed softly. Good thing someone was thinking here.

Cliff was banging around in the medicine cabinet.

"Find what you're looking for?" she called after a moment.

He cursed as a variety of items came crashing down into the sink. "I can't find them."

Annie came in.

Having heard the noises downstairs, Kane loped into the small bathroom, pushing Annie and Cliff closer together.

"Go lie down!"

"I hope you're talking to the dog," Annie murmured wryly.

Kane wandered into the other room and, sighing, took up his usual position at the foot of the bed.

Cliff shook his head, fighting back a smile. What was supposed to be a sizzling morning in bed, more importantly their first, was turning into a nightmare. "I wonder if this is what they call bedroom farce," he grumbled.

He felt Annie closing in behind him, her arms wrapped around his waist, her body conforming to his. The shock, the intimacy of skin against skin, warmed him all over, reminding him they were far from finished.

She felt his buns tighten and grinned. Running her hands up his chest, she watched his nipples peak in the mirror. "You're sexy naked."

"God, I hope so," he said. That elicited a laugh. He held up a foil packet. "Is this what I think it is? I'd hate to be putting on a premoistened towelette."

Annie laughed so hard that her breasts shook against his back.

Cliff stood up straighter. "Do that again."

Their smiles faded as she rubbed slowly against him. "They're so tender they hurt," she said.

"Anything I can do?"

"Kiss them and make them better?"

He handed her the packet over his shoulder. "Ladies first."

She tore it open. Reaching around, her hands did the work, smoothing, fitting, admiring. By the time she finished, he didn't think just kissing would make anything feel better.

"Does that feel right?" she asked.

"I can think of better things to be inside."

Annie pressed her cheek to his back and glimpsed the rumpled bed. They were ready; no turning back now. Maybe fear and uncertainty would always be a part of it, part of the feelings he awoke in her, too strong to be contained any longer.

He turned in her arms, sensing her hesitation. "I don't expect you to say you love me."

"But—"

"Don't say it because it's expected. We're both adults."

Annie promised herself he'd never know how much that hurt. "You haven't even asked and already you know how I feel."

He caressed her cheek. "Just don't decide now. There are things I can do, but I can't be the man I was. Not yet. Until then I can't make you any promises."

"I don't expect any. But they wouldn't change how I feel."

"I wanted to hold off. However," he said, rubbing his belly against hers, "you make that very difficult."

She wanted to argue. Even with her bones melting and her stomach hollow, she wanted to tell him how much he meant to her. She loved him, the anger, the courage, the doubts. But it was a love he wasn't prepared to accept, a love she knew he'd refuse to believe.

"How I feel about you won't change, Cliff." She touched him, there, tracing the tight curls near his manhood. "Let me show you."

She led him toward the bed, but when the tussling was over, he was on top. Stronger, rougher than she'd expected, more demanding and more exhilarating. There were no concessions to his lack of sight now. The movements he made were elemental, primitive, learned before time. The way he reacted when she moved against him, the way he took her breath away.

"Cliff?" A kitten's mew, a woman's insatiable plea. "Keep your hand there. I like the way that feels."

Smells setting off depth charges of desire all their own made him shake down the length of his bow-tight muscles.

And sounds. Her breath catching in the back of her throat, a tattered moan. Those sounds had him coming unglued. Grasping her head with both hands, he kissed her once, softly, and thrust all the way.

He listened and felt. It was like the first time—everything he should have known years ago, the way a woman's body moved, with, against, around, the irresistible places of ecstasy. For a moment he felt awkward. For the first time in weeks he felt in control. For the first time in a lifetime he wasn't alone.

She wrapped her arms around his back. "Come down here and kiss me."

He answered her throaty command. "Then I couldn't do this," he reminded her with his thumb and a slow circle of his hips.

Another gasp. "No, yes, you can do that anytime."

"And would you react like this?" Again, and again she clutched him, arching.

He coiled her hair through his fingers and gently forced her head back to the pillow. She stiffened, unused to any show of force. "Do you like that?" he asked.

She nodded, and he felt her uncertainty, her excitement.

"It's all part of trust. Trust me. Let it go. This is for you."

She believed him, clinging to that as the rush began to build. She was calling his name, bucking, rippling, crying out. Endlessly, mindlessly. And he was with her all the way, in their dark, giving her something he knew no seeing man ever had.

A few minutes, a lifetime... The ripples subsided and she clung to him. He lifted part of his weight off her, leaning on one arm, locked and rigid.

He was shiny with sweat, his head bowed, his hair tousled and damp on his temples. For a second she loved those spikes of dark hair more than she'd loved anything. She wanted to kiss them, comb them, lick them.

She only had to lift her head to kiss his cheek. So she did.

He was breathing heavily, wrung out. And yet with each subsiding tremor inside her, she felt him stiffen, respond, still hard.

"Thank you," she whispered in the shell of his ear.

It was his turn to shudder.

She'd never given herself that completely—no inhibitions, no self-consciousness, nothing but love. Maybe it had something to do with not being watched. Maybe it was how badly she wanted to show him what he meant to her. Sharing was everything. If only she could tell him how free she felt, how totally and absolutely free to love. But his continued silence, his reluctance to resume until he too finished, worried her. "I didn't embarrass you, did I?"

Cliff knew he hadn't finished; he didn't have to. There had been a minute he'd almost given over to it, but he'd held back. Her ecstasy was more important. Now she thought he should be embarrassed. "You mean, because I didn't reach climax?"

"No," she said quickly. "I was kind of wild."

"You were fantastic. I didn't want to," he said, answering his own question. A moment's silence. He laughed hoarsely. "To tell you the truth, I forgot."

"You what?"

"I've never felt a woman do the things you just did. Never paid as much attention, to be honest." Stretching his body the length of hers, he rested against her legs as she drew them together. "I was so wrapped up in you. Are you always that great?"

Only with you, she wanted to answer, touching his hand where it rested on her breast. Somehow her throat was too full with emotions she couldn't express. Had he really paid more attention to her than to himself? That certainly wasn't the sign of the conceited man she'd once feared he was.

He ran his hand down her body, wanting to "see" it, reclining, supine and satisfied. Her skin felt flushed, rosy. He'd done something just for her, and yet she'd done so much for him, opening a whole world of sensation. He wanted to explore every nuance.

"I won't be blind forever," he said.

"I know." Something about that thought nagged at the edges of her contentment. All this could change. But for now his hands were roaming her body unfettered, a garden of sensation.

"It never felt that intense when I could see."

"No?"

Of course, he suspected that had as much to do with how he felt about her as it did with the blindness. But he couldn't tell her that right now.

"Maybe this is my body's way of compensating for lack of sight. Makes it almost worthwhile."

She laughed, and he paused just to feel it. Then he headed toward the bathroom.

Annie watched him walk. "Maybe you'll believe me now when I say you're pretty good just the way you are."

"Another lesson?"

"There are lessons in everything." She trotted after him, wanting to touch him, be near him. "Even if you stayed blind, as long as you accepted yourself, it wouldn't matter." Not to her.

"You know damn well it matters!"

Annie stood in the bathroom doorway, stunned at his outburst.

"Are you trying to tell me something? Have the doctors told you? Is the operation off?"

"No, I—"

"Is it off? Tell me!" He grabbed her arms, not caring if it hurt. He would not be this way forever!

Kane's growl rumbled in the other room. Horseplay was one thing, but even he knew real anger.

Cliff abruptly let her go, turning away. But where could he hide? He wasn't even sure which way he was facing.

"I didn't mean it that way, Cliff."

"You must think I'm a coward, or worse, coming unhinged like that. I don't want to be this way."

She touched him lightly. "You're the bravest man I know."

"Then why am I so scared?"

In the harsh antiseptic light he looked so isolated, so hopeless. But she was there. She reached for him. It didn't solve everything, didn't prevent fear from coiling in her stomach. Making love hadn't broken down every barrier. The way he shut her out was nearly unbearable now that they'd been so close.

Slowly she wrapped her arms around him. "You don't have to be alone," she said. Body to body, she comforted him, as intimate as a man and woman could be. He'd let her inside his deepest fear and she'd blithely told him everything would work out. She cursed herself briefly, but holding Cliff was more important. "I'm sorry I was so callous."

He shook his head but said nothing.

Fear. Intimacy. Sharing. It was part of risking and part of love. You could be hurt most by the things you valued most, the things you let inside. She'd let him in in every way, until everything he felt mattered to her. As for her own doubts and fears, the future would have to wait.

"Will you come back tonight?"

They were standing at the back door. An hour had passed, taken up with getting dressed, talking softly, doing laundry and the sheets from his bed. Emotionally it had been a rocky morning. Cliff knew Annie had a class at two o'clock, but he was reluctant to let her go.

"You could take a shower here, you know."

"I know," she said. "I should have an hour ago when we . . . I will at home."

He reached out and she stepped into his arms.

"I'll be back at six."

"Dave'll be here. We'll have dinner and try to keep our hands off each other."

She hugged him close and tried to land a peck on his cheek. The kiss he caught her with instead had her legs turning rubbery, her bones melting at an alarming rate. "Don't do that tonight," she said, catching her breath, "or we'll have an audience."

"Maybe I'll send him back to the marina," Cliff growled, listening to her steps retreat in the sand.

She should have thought about it during the day. Somehow she made sure she didn't have time. Between showering and dressing, class came and went so swiftly that she was standing at the back door to Cliff and Dave's cottage before she had a chance to really think about what had happened this morning, how their relationship might change.

As it was, in the seconds between ringing the bell and waiting for the door to open, a dozen thoughts and emotions tumbled through her mind.

She loved him—that she knew. He hadn't told her how he felt, but that would come. Judging from his actions this morning, his tenderness and passion, he had to feel something for her. But unless he said so, it remained a closely guarded wish.

And the future?

What would he do when he got his sight back?

What if he didn't? Would he blame her? She who was so quick to say it didn't matter. She cursed once. She'd meant it wouldn't change her feelings for him if he remained blind. Instead she'd come across as a Pollyanna, unsympathetic to his pain.

Sometimes she had such a strong belief in his good qualities that she forgot to have respect for his limitations. He, however, was all too keenly aware of them. She'd have to remember that.

Eight

The door opened.

"Hiya, teach! Come on in."

Dave waved Annie through with a grin and a curious look.

Annie didn't have to look for Cliff; Dave was motioning her toward the living room.

"He's looking at the mail," Dave said, "or holding on to it. Surprised me when I got it out of the box this afternoon. He usually pounces on it the minute the mailman's truck leaves."

Annie stood in the doorway to the living room. Butterflies had taken possession of her stomach; now they took possession of her voice.

Cliff was standing there, hair combed, neatly dressed. She was surprised all over again to see his clean-shaven face, although she'd memorized it, run her palms over it for what had seemed like hours this morning.

If he noticed her, he didn't let on. He was skimming his thumb back and forth over the corner of an envelope. Annie's skin knew exactly what that felt like. She took a deep breath. From here she could just make out the raised black logo. What did it mean?

For the time being she was more concerned with the simple things in life, like how to say hello to a man six hours after making love with him.

She swallowed. "Hello, Cliff."

He started and turned, the tension in his face obvious. There were deep lines around his mouth, lines that hadn't been so noticeable under the beard. The smooth, bare skin brought out the resemblance to Dave and made him look younger, but no less worried.

"Annie." He said her name as if it had been years. Then he took a deep breath of his own, consciously relaxing. The world was right again. He held out one arm and she went to him.

Put off by Cliff's distracted demeanor, self-conscious with Dave there, Annie tried to feel welcome.

Cliff kissed her forehead and rested his cheek there. When he spoke, it was low and meant only for her. "How you doing, honey?"

"Fine."

"No second thoughts?" He squeezed her to his side but never let go of the envelope. "Where's your mouth," he said, momentarily playful.

Annie lifted her face to his. His kiss was warm, slow and deep.

Dave cleared his throat and made sure his presence in the kitchen was known. Way back in the kitchen, by the cupboards and the rattling pots and pans.

"No," Annie said, smiling. "No second thoughts." That she'd ever had doubts was hard to believe. That she'd spent the afternoon alternately worrying and avoiding the future, was irrelevant now. She felt dizzy and half-pulled off her feet. Cliff's iron grip was making sure of that. But it was more. The way he smelled, the way he felt, the body she'd known this morning was beside her again. "And you? Any second thoughts?"

Just that I love you, he almost said. The smile faded. "None. Until this came along." He dropped his arm from around her shoulders.

Annie felt her stomach constrict. "What is it?" She bit her tongue. Obviously he couldn't have read it. "Has Dave seen it?"

"I wouldn't let him open it. I wanted you to be here." He picked up a letter opener, found an opening in the flap and sliced through the envelope so quickly that Annie winced. Then he handed her the contents.

The sound of rustling paper brought Dave, with Kane trailing briskly behind. "What's it say?"

It was from the university hospital, Annie realized, the one that conducted cornea transplants. Her hands shook as she scanned it. She handed it to Dave and sank down on the couch. "I can't—"

Dave started right in. "'Corneas have become ready for implantation... Please check in by three o'clock, Thursday, September twelfth, at the University Medical Center on Carter Road... The operation should take place sometime on the morning of September thirteenth.' That's Friday the thirteenth," he interjected.

Annie groaned. Cliff stood rock-still, listening with his entire body, his jaw clenched so tightly that Annie could count the pulse beats in the vein there.

Dave continued, "'Your doctor has been contacted for all pertinent records and confirms that you are prepared to undergo the transplant procedure... Please call the number below to confirm your arrival...'"

The air was rent with an earsplitting "Yahoo! You're gonna do it, bro!" Dave grabbed Cliff and the men hugged and slapped each other's backs until Annie thought they'd hurt themselves. Dave was unashamedly crying between shouts and laughter.

Annie was crying, too. Everything was happening so fast. Cliff would see again in a matter of days. It was wonderful; she was overjoyed. But it was all too soon. Their relationship was too new. They hadn't had time to even talk about it. If lovemaking could change a relationship irrevocably, what effect would Cliff's regaining his sight have?

"Where is she?" Cliff asked.

"Come on," Dave said.

Annie wiped the tears from her cheeks and laughed in spite of herself. "I didn't want to get crushed!" She let Cliff pull her to him with his free arm. He kissed her quickly, all over her face. She felt Dave tugging to escape Cliff's other arm.

"I'm getting outta here before I get smooched."

"Wise child," Cliff grumbled, giving Dave a shove toward the kitchen. "Get us something to celebrate with."

"Beer's all we've got. Unless you want me to shake up a couple of wine coolers and dump 'em over your head."

"You do and I'll pulverize you," Cliff joked. He turned to Annie, growling in her ear until she quivered from the sheer sensation of it. "And I'll make love to you until the sun comes up, goes down and comes up again. You may not be able to walk for a couple of days. Is that okay with you?"

She nodded, her cheek to his. Her knees went weak. Everything was hitting her at once. How much she loved him, how much she wanted him, how desperately she wanted him to be happy, to be himself again. And how much she wanted him to still love her after the operation. That, more than anything.

"I'll have you right where I want you." He smiled, more dashing and self-assured than ever. "I'll *see* everything." He licked the edge of her ear.

Annie crumbled inside. "Please, please do that."

"Hey, I've got an idea!"

Annie jumped as Dave came back in, beers in hand.

"How about ordering out?"

"Pizza again? This kid lives on pizza," Cliff groused. "Just fix us something in all those pans you're banging around out there."

Annie was abashed to hear herself actually giggle. Cliff kissed her again.

Dave cleared his throat. "I'm not cooking for company. You're the only person I know who deserves my cooking."

"Hey, bud, I've had it up to here with being self-supporting. For the next couple of days you can wait on me hand and foot, fetch my slippers, read me the paper—"

"You don't wear slippers, and if you think I'm going to wait on you, tell it to Kane."

In half an hour dinner was ready, and Annie's sides were sore from laughing. The kitchen became the Cliff and Dave Show, featuring vaudeville routines, corny jokes and plenty of slapstick. "We slice, we dice, we make julienne fries!"

How the spaghetti and salads got to the table intact, much less edible, was a mystery Annie never resolved.

They drank a toast to the future, then Cliff coerced Dave into handling the dishes alone.

"Don't you want to show off for your teacher?" Dave asked facetiously. "Run a couple of loads in the dishwasher?"

"I'm walking my teacher home in the moonlight."

"How do you know there's a moon?" Annie asked.

"You told me last night." He opened the back door, and Kane scooted out in front of them. Cliff took her arm. "Besides, if you're blind, there can be a moon every night."

They walked down the road, their steps scratching in the gravel. With a short command from Cliff, Kane turned around and trotted back to the house. "Catch this, he actually obeyed me," Cliff said.

"Mmm."

"Why so quiet?"

Annie shrugged, smiling apologetically, though she knew it didn't help. "It seems like our little moment has been surpassed."

"You think I'd forgotten making love to you because of that letter?"

"I wouldn't blame you."

He slowed. "Have *you* forgotten?"

"Of course not. It's just that you can put this all behind you now. Go back to your normal life."

"Is that what you want?"

Her throat was so tight that it was painful to speak. She was warring with too many emotions. How many more nights would they have? "I—I just wanted it to last longer, that's all. Before everything went back to the way it was."

He took her in his arms. "It'll be better, Annie. It has to be." In a matter of days he'd see her. He could stop

being this shuttered man and show her the real love he
was capable of. But for now— "We'll see. Just a few
more days."

Was that all she'd have? Lost in her thoughts, Annie
was startled by his next question.

"What time is it?"

She laughed, her body hugged tight to his. She'd
changed clothes from this morning, he noticed. She was
wearing a one-piece sundress, stretchy material that clung
everywhere before flaring to a full skirt that flitted
around his legs. He could tell from the smoothness of her
back that she wasn't wearing a bra. Somehow feeling that
was ten times more exciting than seeing it. "This morning was unbelievable. I'm still not sure I didn't dream it."

"You didn't."

"Are you sore?" he asked.

"No."

His fingertips were on her cheeks. "Are you blush-
ing?"

She laughed again. "That's a very personal question."

"So's this one. What time is it?"

Irritated, she would have stepped back if it weren't for
his arms. "Getting bored already?"

"Hardly. There was something about making love to
you, with my hands and my senses." He ran his hands
possessively down her body.

Her heart went still.

"I'd like to make love to you again."

His body was growing taut and hard, his breath
quickening at the sound of his words and their effect on
Annie. She knew if she put her hand over his heart that
its beat would be like hers, galloping and erratic.

"Is there a moon?"

"Yes."

His hands searched her dress, trying to find the way in. "I want you in the dark, feeling it the way I do." It had buttons; he unbuttoned them, opening it to her waist. He cupped one breast in his hand.

"Are there shadows beside your house?"

"Yes," she gasped as his mouth claimed her. She threw her head back and looked at the moon, the stars, the shadows of the pines on the road.

"I couldn't let you go without showing you one more time how you make me feel."

One more time. It suddenly seemed like enough to last a lifetime, Annie thought, enough to fill a universe to bursting. Her heart was hammering, her legs shaky. Honey started between her legs, hot and sweet. Her doubts shifted like the sand beneath them. No matter how things changed, they'd have this night.

They made it to her house, kissing, clinging, desperate for the one thing each was sure of. She fetched a packing blanket from the studio. There was a sandy spot beside the house, cool and private. The air was brisk on their skin as they removed their clothes.

It was pitch-black. She had to rely on her hearing to know exactly where he was. When he came closer, she sensed his presence before she felt him, masculine, powerful, ominous in the dark. Naked to the sky, buffeted by the night breeze, they were like strangers, bodies meeting in the dark. His hand on her breast was electric, her response instantaneous.

"What if someone sees?" she asked with her last shred of common sense.

"What if they do?" he replied gruffly. Coaxing her to him, he made it clear he didn't give a damn about anyone but them and the love they were going to make.

He found her tension with his fingers, massaging, easing, reading her body the way no man had, lowering her. The blanket was scratchy against her back, the sand pliant as they moved to accommodate each other, caressing each other's special places. A wash of emotion and rhythm rose and receded and rose again, joining their hurried breath and urgent words. The waves whispered and rolled with them.

It was different in the dark. The feel of skin, smooth and taut, pulsing, covered with fine goose bumps. Slick hair, the taste of a mouth, the fine stubble of a beard already growing back. She teased, tasted and vowed to remember. If there were lonely nights to come, they wouldn't be empty of memories.

And when it was over for him, she responded to every aftershock with the only words that mattered— "I love you." She touched his face once more and said, "I love you." She ran her hands through his still-long hair and said, "I love you," all the while knowing none of the memories would ever be enough if he left her.

His entire body shuddered as he rested his chin on her shoulder, exhausted. He felt her quivering around him. Kissing her cheek, he felt the wetness. "Are you crying?"

Her body trembled. There was no hiding from him, not even in the dark. Hot tears ran down her cheeks and into her hair. "I'm sorry. I didn't mean to."

"Why?"

She tried to laugh. "Too much emotion, maybe."

He cursed softly. "Annie, it was wonderful. Tell me."

Maybe it was too wonderful. She shook her head. "Don't make me explain it. I love you, that's all. I'm sorry."

He kissed the salt on her lips, the puffiness under her eyes.

"Don't. I look terrible when I cry." She hastily wiped her tears with the back of her hand and sniffed.

"You look beautiful," he said with complete sincerity. "And you taste even better." He licked her cheek, placing tiny open kisses on her lashes. "Mmm, salty."

She stroked his back, his neck, the plastic of his sunglasses. "First you lose the beard, next these. When the sun comes up, I won't even recognize you."

"I'll recognize you."

And how would he look at her then?

Both were lost in thought for minutes. When Cliff withdrew, they lay side by side. Picking up a corner of the blanket, he covered them, then surprised himself by saying something he'd been thinking all evening. "Come to the hospital with me."

She huddled in closer to him. "I thought you'd want to go it alone."

"So did I." She understood him a lot better than he'd realized. It was scary. After all, if she was there when the bandages came off, she might be there when they told him the operation hadn't worked. How would he say goodbye to her then? How avoid her pity?

He hugged her to him, warming her back with his front. Nothing was going to go wrong. This nightmare would end, and Annie would be waiting for him on the other side. Only then could they make promises, plan a future together. Only then would he be able to say the words that she'd said to him tonight. *I love you.* "I want you there when I wake up," he said.

She touched his hand where it rested on her breast, signaling her assent.

"Of course, if we sleep out here all night, we may never wake up," he joked past the lump in his throat. "It's freezing out here!'' He gave her fanny a smack. ''Last one in the house is a rotten egg!''

Annie jumped up after him, kicking around in the sand for their pile of clothes. ''You'd desert a naked defenseless woman in the middle of the wild outdoors—''

''Not ten feet from her own house—''

''What's worse, you probably can't even find the door!'' She shook out the blanket and tossed him a scrunched handful of discarded clothing.

''I can find the deck on the beachside,'' he retorted.

''With your shin, maybe.''

''That does it. I've been insulted enough.'' He made a lunge for her.

Because she hadn't expected it, he almost caught her. ''What are you doing?''

''That's it. Say something so I can find you.''

Annie backed up, the blanket clutched to her chest. ''I'm not going to say anything.''

''Aha! That's all I needed.''

He lunged again, and she jumped out of his way, backing cautiously toward the deck. ''What are you going to do if you catch me?''

''For beginners, I thought I might toss you into the surf. That'll teach you to tease a blind man. Now, where are you, hussy?''

One lunge to the left, one squeal as he caught her arm, and then she slipped agilely out of his grasp. In a few steps she was up on the deck sliding the doors open. ''Last one in is a rotten egg.''

Cliff rammed his shin against the planking and let out a curt expletive. ''I'd settle for last one in the shower,'' he muttered blackly, rubbing his leg.

''Oh, Mr. Sullivan-n-n-n,'' she cooed.

Her throaty voice made chills run up his spine. Not to mention the fact he was sitting there plumb naked on a freezing September night in northern Michigan. "Yes, Ms. Rosetti?"

"How about if we both head for the shower?"

He found the steps and limped across the deck to the sliding doors. "I thought you'd never ask."

Sitting in the hospital corridor, Annie remembered that night. She was keenly aware that she and Cliff had been lovers for no more than one complete day. In the shower his body hair had looked black as it had stuck wet and clinging to his body. The way she had, pressing soft kisses to his throat.

She hugged herself and leaned back in a plastic molded chair that certainly must have been designed for human beings shaped differently than she. Amazing that a hospital would provide something so completely unsuited to the human form, she groused as she watched another nurse parade by.

Dave sat hunched forward, staring disconsolately at the blue, green, yellow and red tape leading up and down the linoleum, heaven knows where. Who'd come up with this system anyway? And who was the poor lug who'd spent all that time on his hands and knees laying it out? Dave would have gotten right down beside him if it would make this wait go any faster.

Cliff, being Cliff, was determined to go it alone. They shouldn't have been surprised. They'd checked him in last night and arrived this morning to find the operation already in progress. He wanted them here, but he'd lied about when it was scheduled. Dave planned to throttle him.

In twenty-four hours the bandages would come off, and they'd know the results. "When he's better, *I'm* going to pulverize him," Dave muttered darkly.

Annie laughed softly. "It'll work out."

"A high success rate for a transplant," Dave said, repeating the doctor's words. "Miracle of modern science."

Annie nodded, then retreated to her own thoughts about miracles. Like love itself. She reminded herself that "I love you" was no magic phrase. On the other hand, if Cliff had only said it the last time they'd made love, she'd be holding on to it with all her heart right now.

Smelling hospital coffee, Annie opened her eyes. "Thanks." She took another Styrofoam cup from Dave. He needed to be up and walking around. This was the fourth cup he'd brought her. She would have preferred herbal tea. "I was just going to ask you to get me another," she lied.

"Bullfeathers. You didn't even know I was gone."

She shook her head sheepishly and smiled. "True."

The elevator door squeaked open. Annie was beginning to hate that squeak. Dave was on the verge of finding an oil can and fixing it himself. Then they recognized the doctor and knew it was Cliff's stretcher. Within moments they were beside it.

"Cliff?"

His face swathed in bandages, he turned his head on the flat pillow. "Annie?" He sounded groggy, and his hand was limp as it rose.

"I'm here," she said, grasping his hand until she felt a returning squeeze.

"You're not supposed to be here," he muttered. "I sent you away for the morning."

"Wild horses wouldn't keep us away, and you know it."

"Yeah, whose bright idea was it to lie about the operation, huh?"

"Dave," Annie shushed.

"Dave," Cliff muttered, lifting his other hand before he faded out and it dropped back to the sheets.

A nurse stepped between them to jockey the gurney into his room. "He'll need some time to recoup, then he'll have a splitting headache. A couple of hours ought to do it. In twenty-four hours we'll remove the bandages."

"You're sure?" Dave insisted.

"Promise," she said, stripping off the green operating uniform.

"Annie?"

"I'm here, Cliff."

He said nothing for a moment, a faint smile on his lips, her hand clutched in his. He lifted it to his lips and kissed it. "I knew it was you in the corridor. I heard your bracelets."

She laughed. "Are they that loud?"

"When your head is pounding, they are."

"I'm sorry."

She made a move to remove them, but that required his letting go of her hand, which he wasn't about to do.

"I love you," he mumbled.

Her heart stopped. "What?"

"Excuse me." The other nurse bustled in. "He's quite groggy. Perhaps you could come back tonight."

Annie realized Cliff was already asleep, his hand limp in hers. Reluctantly she released it. The nurse was right. She couldn't pin her heart on words spoken so soon after surgery. No matter how badly she wanted to.

Nine

After two years in college, Ann Arbor was home to Dave, so when an uncomfortable and grumpy Cliff kicked them out of his hospital room the next morning, Dave showed Annie the sights.

She saw the University of Michigan, the library, the student union, the bookstores and the stadium. It was stop-and-go all the way with September's returning students crossing everywhere but at the lights and furniture-stacked Volvos double-parked outside student apartments.

"That's mine, top floor right," Dave said, pointing as they drove by yet another brick house.

"Oh," Annie said, secretly wishing they'd taken a vigorous walk instead. Obviously Dave needed to drive the way Cliff needed to run, Annie realized, missing her miles of Lake Michigan beach.

More by habit than thought, Dave pulled up in front of Bell's Pizza. "Want some?"

"Don't think I've ever had a more gracious invitation," Annie said wryly.

Dave skimmed over the sarcasm, reciting the doctor's optimistic prognosis once more. "He should be able to see immediately after the bandages come off. Hell, he could drive back home."

"Please," Annie said, laughing. "I had to ride in that boat with him."

"Okay, maybe not drive, but within a week or two, with glasses. Miracles of modern science, eh?"

"Yeah. Just keep repeating that."

They ordered. And waited.

"I'm going to get a microwave," Annie said. "I'm beginning to hate waiting for anything."

"Know how you feel."

Annie played with a paper napkin, wishing she had some good firm clay to keep her hands busy. "When he's better, he'll be going back to work, won't he?" There it was, the big question. She looked across at Dave.

He shrugged and leaned back in his seat, his legs halfway out in the aisle. "Doc said it could be soon. What's his name again?"

"Dr. Tanarawanda or something like that. I can't pronounce it."

"Whew. Glad I'm not the only one."

"So," she said, wondering if he'd changed the subject on purpose, "about Cliff's job. He is planning on going back to the Upper Peninsula?"

Her concern finally dawned on Dave. "He hasn't talked it over with you?"

"He's been waiting for the operation," she said, gazing at the Formica.

Dave muttered a curse. "Pardon my French, but sensitivity doesn't exactly run in our family. Maybe that comes from being a family of men. I don't know. We don't always say what we mean."

Annie left off playing with a plastic fork and clenched her hands in her lap. "Cliff's had enough experience with women. You'd think he'd have learned long ago how to say what they wanted to hear."

Dave winced. "Oh, the ladies. Well, you know Cliff."

"Do I?"

"Sure, he used to play the playboy, but he's subtler now." Dave grimaced at how that came out. "He's nowhere near as wild as I remember."

"That could be because of the accident," she pointed out.

"I think it's because of you." He hoped he wasn't letting everything out of the bag. He'd seen the effect Annie had on his brother. Blindness or no, Cliff was climbing the walls, pacing the floor and practically chewing nails over this woman. If anybody ought to tell her Cliff loved her, it should be Cliff. Hell, it should be obvious to both of them.

"That's okay," Annie said. She sighed and tossed him a forgiving look. Lifting a slice of pizza from the box, she cut the stringy cheese with her fingers. "I should be talking this over with Cliff, not you."

Dave pulled his legs in quickly as a coed with a carryout order walked by. He was so rangy, Annie noticed, more so than Cliff, who was more self-contained. In a lot of ways.

"You know," Dave said, downing half a Coke, "I don't know how much this means, but when Mom was sick, Cliff shielded me from just about everything. I was only five then, but I think I would have liked to know

more of what was going on. He doesn't see it that way.
He takes everything on himself, doesn't share his troubles. That's his way of protecting the people he cares
about.''

"Thanks for including me in that." Annie touched his
arm.

Dave munched a crust, then dropped it into the box
with a clunk. "Yeah, but what happens when he shuts
out the people he's trying to protect?''

Annie realized she wasn't the only one hurt by Cliff's
determination to go it alone. "It'll be okay. You'll have
your brother back good as new.''

When they returned to the hospital, Cliff was sitting up
in bed. Dr. T, as Dave had taken to calling him, was on
the far side of the bed. A nurse was wadding up discarded bandages.

The bandages were off.

The sunglasses on.

"Leave those on to prevent any accidental touching or
bumping of the eyes," the doctor was saying. His soothing voice with its lilting East Indian accent carried across
the room.

Cliff's head turned. Standing frozen in the doorway,
Annie wished that sausage pizza had been milder. Her
stomach was doing cartwheels. The bandages were off!

She silenced the bracelets that were swaying and clattering on her left wrist. A hundred questions rushed
through her mind. Had he heard them come in? Had he
seen them? Was he looking at her right now? It couldn't
be bad news, could it? She wanted to rush to his bedside
and hold him. She couldn't move.

He muttered a blunt, "Excuse me," turned his back on
them and swung his legs over the edge. Pacing the length

of the bed, he turned and came toward her. This time, unlike any way she'd ever seen him walk, he hesitated.

He didn't have to ask if it was her. Something about the way she held her hands in front of her, those bracelets; the color of her sweater alone stung his sensitive eyes.

She was blurry but getting clearer. He had to get closer to see the look in her eyes.

His chest was bare, Annie thought irrelevantly. Having refused to wear "that asinine hospital gown," he was wearing blue boxer shorts, the same ones she'd helped toss in countless loads of laundry these past few weeks. His legs were powerful-looking as always, darkened with gold and brown hairs. Really, he wasn't wearing anything less than he wore on the beach. But coming toward her, in the harsh hospital light, he looked half-naked and vulnerable.

She concentrated on all those things. Anything to take her mind off the petrifying fact that he was looking right at her.

He stopped in front of her, so close she had to look up. That's when her eyes began to fill with tears. She blinked them back; she *had* to know. "Can you—" She choked on the tightness in her throat.

Up close, she was still blurry. He wanted to blink, but he was afraid she'd disappear. She was shorter than he'd pictured, maybe because she was standing beside Dave. Her hair was medium brown, her sweater a riot of purples and pinks and blues. He heard the bracelets tinkle as she wiped something from her cheek. He touched her shoulders, the fuzzy rough weave of the hand-loomed sweater familiar to his fingers. "You've worn this before."

She nodded.

Funny that he had to touch her, hear her, to confirm what his eyes could see.

"Can you see me?" she whispered, knowing it was true. All he had to do was say the words.

He touched her hair instead. That's how it all began, wasn't it, him touching her hair? There were combs holding it off her face on both sides. He saw the glint of copper, felt its coolness. Her hair *was* frizzy, wild and curly, more erotic than he'd imagined. His fingers got caught in it. He wanted to joke about it, but even through the gauziness that remained he could see traces of uncertainty in her eyes.

How often had that been there without his knowing? How often had he hurt her unintentionally while wrapped up in his own problems? "How often have you looked at me like that and I've been too blind to see it?"

"Cliff!"

He found her mouth, or she found his. With their arms wrapped around each other, it wasn't hard. He crushed her to him, wishing he could take back every irritable moment, every moment they'd wasted not laughing and touching and holding each other just like this. "Annie, honey..."

Dave pumped the doctor's hand, subjecting him to the same kind of hugs and backslaps he would have traded with Cliff had his brother not had something better to do with his arms.

Annie was pounding Cliff's back with fists of her own. "Why didn't you tell us the bandages were coming off so soon? The nurse promised us—"

"I strong-armed the doctor into taking them off early. I didn't want to drag you through it."

She took his face firmly in her hands. "Damn it, when are you going to realize you can share the bad things, too? That's what we're here for."

"Shh. It doesn't matter now." He took her face in his hands instead. "You're fuzzy. You know that?"

She laughed and sniffled.

"Some lenses, perhaps," the doctor interrupted, eager to escape Dave's exuberant embrace, "after the sight has stabilized. Although the initial blurriness should fade within the week."

"This is fine, Doc," Cliff murmured, looking down into Annie's face. "In fact, it's about the most beautiful thing I've ever seen."

Annie made herself smile, not sure she could believe him precisely because she wanted to so badly.

"I probably look terrible," Cliff said, reaching for his sunglasses. "But do you mind if I take these off?"

She swallowed and shook her head. She wouldn't have minded being shanghaied to China right now, as long as he was with her.

He reached past her to flick the light switch, the cloudy day outside providing the only light in the room. Keeping his back to the window, Cliff slowly took off his sunglasses.

"His eyes will be red for a few days," the doctor said.

Annie saw that for herself. The part that should have been white was indeed red and painful-looking. She grimaced, and Cliff hurriedly began to put his glasses back on.

"No," she said, softly touching his arm, "they look like they hurt, that's all."

It was his turn to shake his head. "Not much."

She knew he wouldn't admit it if they did, but at the moment it didn't matter. The eyes that stared so seriously into hers were brown with gold and hazel highlights. Black circles darkened the skin around them. She traced them with shaking fingertips.

"From the operation," Cliff said. "I look like I just went ten rounds with Sugar Ray."

"You look like you're gonna have one hell of a hangover," Dave chortled.

Cliff looked at his younger brother, at Annie, and back again. "I shouldn't have dragged you two through all this."

"Yeah, right, sure," Dave replied. "Like we're going to hand you a bus ticket and say, 'Call when the operation's over.'"

Cliff laughed and surreptitiously wiped what looked like a tear off his cheek as he put his glasses on. "One of the symptoms, right, Doc?"

"Yes, Mr. Sullivan. That is right. You may have tearing."

"Bull!" Dave said succinctly.

"Come here." Cliff grabbed him and held on tight. "Have you been taking care of this lady?"

"Like you said."

"Better than you took care of me, I hope."

"She's not as grumpy."

"She's better looking, too."

"About time you wised up."

"Don't get smart. I can reach you now." Cliff playfully swatted Dave's shoulder. Dave made a fist to hit back.

"Ah," the doctor warned, "do not hit a recovering patient."

Dave grabbed a tissue off the nightstand and blew his nose loudly. "Hey, why don't we go somewhere and really party?"

"And make a fool of myself in public like I did at that barbershop?" Cliff retorted. "No thanks. No more public performances for me. This has been nightmare enough."

Nightmare, Annie thought dully. As if all her teaching had brought him nothing but humiliation. She shook off the feeling as Cliff threw an arm around her shoulders and gave her a quick squeeze.

"This thing is almost over. I'll be me again."

She understood what Cliff meant, really she did. He meant the blindness and all its frustrations would be over. Not *them*. The pep talk, for what it was, failed to lift her plummeting spirits. She'd spent so much time with him, given him pieces of herself, pieces he seemed suddenly eager to discard.

"Please, you may all come to my office when you're ready. I have some instructions I would like to give."

"Sure, Doc," Cliff said. Then, as he put on his hospital gown, saying, "The last time I wear one of these monstrosities," he spelled out what a miserable couple of months it had been. Annie stood loyally by, the smile on her face feeling more false and brittle as the minutes ticked on.

"Now where's the doc's office?" Cliff finally asked.

"Down here," Dave replied.

"You two go," Annie said. "I'm going to stop off in the ladies' room for a minute." She sidestepped Cliff's embrace and took a quick left turn.

He felt that all too familiar frustration ramming home again. Damn it, why didn't seeing help? Something was wrong with Annie and he didn't know what it was. At least this time he could catch up to her before the door closed. "Anything wrong?"

"I cried so hard I ruined my makeup, that's all." She wouldn't ruin this day for him for all the tea in China. She just had to get away, anywhere, alone.

As the washroom door closed behind her, she rested her forehead against the cool green tile. She was being petty and insecure. Stupid. Infantile. "And to top it off, I'm wallowing in self-accusations." This was probably Cliff's happiest moment. Why did she feel kicked in the stomach? Just because he couldn't wait to forget everything they'd been through together?

Splashes of cold water did wonders for her face but nothing for her stomach. *Get ready to let him go,* the puffy-eyed woman in the mirror said. No crying, no clinging. She'd tried both with Ken; she hadn't even escaped with her dignity. Not this time. She loved Cliff with everything she had; she always would. She wouldn't cheapen it by clinging when he wanted to leave. He was going back to his old life. He made it very clear that was all he'd ever wanted.

Annie fixed her lipstick, wasted minutes trying to apply eyeliner to wet eyelids, then went looking for the doctor's office.

Except for the unpronounceable name on the door, Annie knew she'd never remember anything about Dr. T's office—just Dave perched on the radiator and Cliff sitting in a leather chair, reaching out for her hand as the doctor issued his instructions.

Tiny shivers ran up and down her every time she caught Cliff glancing her way. Knowing he could see her was both terrifying and exciting. He was hers, for these few moments at least. She forced a smile. Nothing, not even her own doubts, were going to spoil this day.

The doctor cleared his throat. "The symptoms you have now should subside. Meanwhile, you must call us immediately if there are any signs of rejection."

"Right," Cliff said.

"We have a saying here, RSVP. That means four things. *R* is for redness. That is a sign of a rejection episode."

"I already have that," Cliff said, his attention riveted on the doctor. The man was talking failure. Cliff had no intention of failing. Not now.

"I know. I mean the redness that returns. This will fade soon."

"And the other three letters?"

"*S* for soreness, *V* for vision change—"

"It's going to change every day. You told me that."

"It should improve. If for any reason it gets quickly worse, call immediately. We sometimes can treat the eyes with steroid drops and the rejection reverses without surgery."

"And *P*?"

"Photophobia."

"What's that?" Dave chirped.

"Means I hate having my picture taken," Cliff retorted. He squeezed Annie's hand, and she glanced over. That was when he remembered she could see him as well as he could see her. He'd have to be careful what he showed here. He didn't want her worrying. He let go of her hand and crossed his arms, trying to look casual. "Rejection is a faint possibility, isn't it? I mean the success rate is very good."

"Oh, it's excellent, and rejection can be treated."

"And there could be another transplant."

"Yes, we could go so far as a tissue-matching program to ensure even greater success. As long as the eyes aren't damaged by the rejection itself...."

Cliff's mouth was tight, so he purposely relaxed it. He wanted Annie. He wanted out of this mess once and for all. He wanted to get on with his life, with their lives. Above all, he wanted to erase the worry that was on her face when she'd come in. She shouldn't have to be put through this. "How long before I can be certain this operation is going to take?"

"A month is advisable."

"A month," Cliff said flatly.

"Yes."

"When can I go back to work?"

"Well," the doctor dawdled, his gold pen hovering over Cliff's chart. "If this is correct about what you do for a living, I think it would be advisable that you wait until we can fit you with prescriptive lenses—"

"You mean glasses?"

"Or contact lenses. In addition, it is not uncommon to continue to be photophobic to a greater or lesser degree, almost indefinitely."

"Meaning?" Cliff barked.

"Meaning," the doctor hurried on, cognizant of the growing tension in the room, "you may find you need sunglasses on any bright day."

"Luckily he looks sexy in sunglasses," Annie mentioned, smoothing the waters.

Cliff stopped frowning long enough to glance her way. This gnawing frustration was supposed to have ended with the operation. As long as there was any possibility things could go wrong, there would be only more waiting ahead. How long could he keep them both walking this tightrope?

Annie smiled, squeezing his hand. "It'll be fine."

Not for the first time, he prayed it would.

The next two weeks flew by, Annie's doubts withering like autumn leaves. She couldn't stop watching Cliff, and the feeling seemed mutual. Every time they walked on the beach, stopping for a sunset or a sea gull in flight, she caught him looking at her.

Every night they made love.

"Let me see," he breathed, turning her insides to soft flowing honey, her heartbeat to pounding waves. By turns intense then mild, his hands roved over her, his dark brown eyes greedy for everything the light of the bedside lamp revealed.

Annie watched, too. This was another Cliff, a Cliff she'd seen in pieces, never whole. Stubborn and precise, often egotistically pleased with himself for having captured such a beautiful woman while blind.

With very little effort, she could forget her fears and simply treasure each day, refusing to count the days until their month was up. Dave was back in school. They had time together. Time was all they needed. Cliff was restless without work, his vision too blurry to read. He strode the beaches, jogging and working out while Annie taught at the hospital. Today she was stealing a few morning hours to build up her pottery inventory. Her days were booked and her nights had become so full....

"Hi!" Cliff called.

Annie's heart jumped. No matter how many times she saw him, she was helpless against that reaction.

Jogging up from the water's edge, he stopped in the shade of the open garage door. He balanced his sunglasses on his head. "Hot day."

"Isn't it wonderful?"

He grinned one of those "eat your heart out" grins that turned her to jelly, then stripped off his T-shirt in one move, leaving nothing but his blue nylon running shorts, his running shoes and a body glistening with sweat. Although she knew every inch of that body, it never ceased to affect her in the most elemental ways. A sear of desire and a flush of modesty overtook her. She felt the urge to tug up the strap of her sundress as it slouched down her shoulder, but her hands were covered with clay.

Kane, less impressed by his master, flopped down on the cool concrete.

"You're wearing that dog out," Annie scolded.

"He needs the exercise."

"You mean you do."

"But my dear, I have you."

Annie poked him in the ribs with her elbow while accepting a chaste kiss on the cheek.

It certainly was a glorious Indian summer morning, one of those rare end-of-September days, precious because you knew they couldn't last. Annie pondered that thought, watching a pot spin. Can't last, can't last, it whispered.

Cliff toyed with her strap and the skin beneath. Lord, she was sexy. "Got a towel I could borrow, pretty lady?"

"Under the sink."

He found one in a cupboard built under the workbench, rinsing his whole head under the arched faucet before briskly toweling off. "You look good," he said, one hip against the counter.

So did he. Annie shrugged and went back to her pottery. "Don't look too long. I have work to catch up on."

"Am I keeping you too busy? Nights, I mean?"

She tugged down the corners of her mouth coquettishly. "My nights are fine. Wonderful, in fact."

He grinned, swaggering without moving a muscle.

"Did I say that was all your doing?" she replied with a huff.

"Come across a good book then?"

She pursed her lips. "I didn't say that."

"Could be," he said, shrugging, "if that book was *The Joy of Sex*."

Was that all it was to him? She looked startled, then hurt, then angry that he'd caught it.

Cliff swore under his breath. That had been a stupid, macho thing to say. Anything for a quip. He puttered with the shelves. A month, the doctor said. Two more lousy weeks. Cliff couldn't make promises until he was sure, no matter how badly he wanted to. "I know what you want me to say, Annie. We should talk about some kind of future, but I can't, not yet."

"Then don't," she said, stung. "It's not as if I'm pressuring you."

"No, but I hear it loud and clear. You want commitment. You want something I can't give."

Was this it then, the beginning of the end? Annie felt her hands wavering on the clay. She lifted them off, not wanting to destroy something she'd created, something special. "Could we not talk about this now?"

Cliff kicked himself for treating her reasonable expectation like an unwelcome obligation. She wasn't the only one who longed for a life together. "I shouldn't have yelled." He dragged a hand over his slick neck. "Mind if I use your shower?"

"Not at all." She was frosty.

He was thirsty. "I'm gonna grab a drink in the kitchen."

"Fine."

The door to the house closed. Kane looked up to watch his master leave.

"It's okay, boy. He'll be back," Annie said quietly. But how many more times?

Yes, she wanted more. If Cliff couldn't give it, better to settle it now than go on pretending. Unfortunately there would never be a good time to let go. Far from pressing him, she had to let him know he was free.

Cliff returned, his shorts clinging to him in damp places that made her heart beat dull and hard, adding to the pain.

"When are you going back to work?" she asked without emotion.

"Up north?"

She nodded.

"When the doctors give me the go-ahead. The mine requires a doctor's slip. So do all the other authorities. There'll be a battery of tests, no doubt." If only she'd wait.

"You'll be leaving then."

"I have to work for a living, Annie. Lord knows I can't do pottery."

She involuntary glanced at the shelves, her eyes going to the half-dozen pieces he'd made. Why was she doing this? Why ruin their few remaining days? "I like that tall one you made."

"Not bad," he said, coming slowly toward her.

"No, it isn't," she replied, trying to sound cool, feeling the heat still coiled in his body. "At least I taught you something." She got up, avoiding him, lifting the new piece off the wheel. She set it carefully on the shelf, as if it held someone's heart.

Cliff was behind her, running his fingertips across her bare back. "You taught me a whole way of life," he murmured. That way of life included her. If things turned out the way he wanted, it always would. Of course, she could say no, especially to living that far north.

He withdrew his hand and thought things out. The hospital in Marquette might not have any need for an art therapist. Traveling to art fairs would be an extra three hours away. Maybe she didn't want to go. Was this her way of putting him off?

"Will you come visit me?" he asked. He wouldn't insist on an answer now. She could check it out, make a decision when she'd seen the place.

Visit? The word tore a small hole in her heart. "It's a long drive," she hedged. "It'll be longer once the snow hits."

Winters. Linda had hated that prospect, too, Cliff remembered, when she'd turned down his proposal of marriage. It wasn't a question a man asked many times in his life. He wasn't about to stand here and watch his dreams crumble.

It wasn't fair—it didn't resolve the argument—but he reached up anyway, his fingers dancing through the chimes. They sounded through his pulse and echoed in the large room, musical, sensual.

Annie turned as if called, not surprised by the intensity in his eyes.

"They still sound like you," he said.

Ten

─────

Annie flushed. The room felt hot and dry, like the inside of a kiln.

Cliff approached, backing her up against the wall.

Her eyes pleaded with him. She needed reassurance, some idea that he planned to stay, at least keep her in his life. "Making love doesn't solve arguments."

"Yes, but do you notice how few start when you are?"

She held up clay-crusted hands. "I can't touch you."

He pressed in against her with his body, hot, hard, the concrete block wall at her back cold and just as hard. "Have you ever done it with no hands?" His smile was cockier than ever, belying whatever troubled his eyes.

She shook her head. "Somebody's got to—"

The thought went unfinished as he lifted her hands, pinning them to the wall with his, the clay and water oozing between their entwined fingers. The subtle circling of his hips became a not-so-subtle pumping motion that made her knees weak, her own rhythm ignite.

One small voice said they had to talk; she couldn't surrender like this every time he—

His mouth covered her ear, and her knees buckled. Her voice cracked when she tried to speak. "Won't it be hard to take our clothes off?"

"If we don't, I'm going to be mighty embarrassed."

She gave a throaty laugh just as he laved her neck with his tongue.

If she had any idea how close he was... "You wear this when you throw clay. That means you can get it dirty," he reasoned bluntly.

"Not fair getting logical when you're making me crazy." It was her turn to nibble his ear. "How about if I run my hands through your hair?"

"No!" He jumped back.

"Vain."

"I just showered."

She came at him slowly, hands reaching. "So shower again."

"Annie," he warned. He made a motion to run his hand through his hair. Catching sight of a palm full of grayish clay made him stop just in time. He rolled his eyes.

He rolled his eyes.

Annie stopped. She'd never seen him do that before, so rarely did she see him without his sunglasses even now. How could he leave when she was still learning him?

"How *are* we supposed to do this?" he said.

She sighed and looked out the open doors toward the beach. "There are still tourists hanging around. Maybe we'd better wait."

Waiting. That was his line.

Annie watched emotions she didn't recognize flicker across his face. Frustration and anger, she recognized, not the others. She was willing to wait out the silence this time, but he said nothing, turning to rinse his hands in the sink.

"When's your next art fair?" he asked out of the blue.

"Next week, a Christmas bazaar at the high school."

"Christmas, it's barely October!"

She shrugged. "It's in town, so I'll go for the day."

"Can I come?"

"As I recall you were bored last time," she remarked dryly.

"I want to *see* one. I should be more help."

Buoyed that he wanted to take part in something so central to her life, eager for the chance to spend as much time with him as possible, Annie nodded.

"Kane."

The dog ambled over. Cliff picked up his harness.

"You never used that when you were blind. You always insisted on the leash."

"When I was blind, I didn't want to look it. Anyway this keeps him from straining so hard."

"We should talk."

Cliff paused in the doorway. "Wouldn't it be easier to take it as it comes?" He looked at her gently, pausing on the edge of the sand.

And when it goes? she thought.

She watched him walk toward his house. She had to give him space, time to get used to everyday life again. There was love there, she knew it. That he hadn't spoken it, that he was letting their days dwindle, made her wonder about their future, and more determined than ever to seize the present.

* * *

A week passed. A week of sweetest attention from Cliff. In a restaurant atop a hotel he ignored every beautiful woman present, teasingly admitting, "Of course, I can't exactly see them in this candlelight."

Chuckling, Annie held the menu closer to the candle and surreptitiously read it to him. At least he could do without the sunglasses here.

But for the past few evenings they'd begun drifting, unsure of what to say, tiptoeing around feelings each was afraid to confront. Annie decided tonight was the night. She couldn't be true to her feelings if she didn't directly confront Cliff about his.

Picking up Chinese food in town, she got to his house at six.

Cliff stepped away from the back to let her enter, replacing the lid on a bubbling pot of spaghetti sauce. "We must have crossed wires somewhere." He stacked the take-out boxes on the counter and gave her a peck on the cheek.

"Perfect example of a lack of communication," she replied stiffly.

Cliff let that one drop, like a stone. "Wine with dinner?"

As they sat on the living room sofa afterward, Cliff congratulated himself on at least getting the fire to crackle. Dinner had been a feast of tension and strained silence.

"Are we ready now?" He set a glass of wine in front of her.

"I thought you weren't supposed to drink," she said. This discussion could be the turning point of their entire relationship. Suddenly she wanted to put it off as long as possible. "The doctor said something about it constricting the blood vessels."

Cliff pursed his lips, feeling strangely touched. "For someone who never stopped staring at me while we were in his office, you heard every word he said." He lifted the solitary glass in a salute to her. "Just a sip, then it's yours."

Annie watched him savor it, seeing his mouth move, imagining his tongue and the dark taste of red wine. Heady, intoxicating. "Potent," she said aloud.

He glanced at her, sunglasses off, brown eyes darkening. Then he threw back his head and laughed. "We know where your mind is."

Coloring, she didn't bother to protest.

He leaned back, comfortably placing an arm around her shoulders. "Have I told you how lucky I am to have found you?"

"Only a few hundred times. And only since you've seen what it is you found."

"No!"

"You never mentioned it before the operation."

"I didn't want to count my blessings before they hatched, or something like that. You thought I was waiting to check you out? Sorry, honey, you're confusing me with another vacuous SOB." This time he took a longer swallow from her glass.

Annie squeezed her eyes shut, denouncing herself silently. "I'm sorry, Cliff. We shouldn't judge people according to the past."

"It's normal enough," he said, sighing. "You know, this doesn't have to be a knockdown, drag-out, souls-bared kind of night. Just come at me with it. What's worrying you?"

Annie sipped and studied the flames. "I love you."

He nodded and let that sink in. "I wanted to wait until I knew about my eyes. I have this thing about supporting my family. Good eyesight is necessary for setting charges, any kind of blasting."

"I can imagine," she said, something shivering inside her. "Is it dangerous work? I mean, look what happened before."

"That was an accident. Won't happen again."

She touched his cheek without thinking. It seemed like anything she did lately was thought out, careful. Why not say what she was thinking? "I like you without your sunglasses."

"I can't look directly into the fire, but I can look at you."

"So I noticed." There hadn't been a day, or night, when she hadn't caught him doing just that. "You look neater without the beard. Not so dissolute."

"That should impress the people from the Bureau of Mines. Don't want 'em thinking I was on a month-long bender." He waited for her laughter to subside. "We're being honest here?" he asked, nuzzling her hair. "There's been a reason I haven't said I love you, although I've loved you quite a while."

Her heart stopped, anticipating.

"I wanted to be free of this worry."

"I understand that."

"I was so wrapped up in my own problems I never realized how badly you might want to hear it."

"That's all right. You've already said it."

"I have? When?"

Her eyes twinkled. "In the hospital."

He'd thought it. Lord, how he'd thought it. But he couldn't actually remember. "When?"

She gave his ribs a good poke. "When you were coming out of surgery and still under the anesthetic. I ought to hit you with one of these pillows for putting me through all that. I understand not wanting to make promises when you don't know the future, but who does? If you love someone, you should tell them. No guarantees, and no, I'm not crowding you, but if you do love me, I'd appreciate knowing how you feel!"

"Simmer down."

"Don't patronize me."

He laughed instead. "How often have you wagged that finger at me when I couldn't see it?" He took her in his arms, clearly enjoying the resistance she put up. "You have a lot of the schoolmarm in you, teach."

"I take it that's not a compliment."

He kissed her nose, insinuating his body next to hers. "As a potter, though, I must say you have great hands." He cupped her bottom and drew her even closer. "Not to mention your creativity."

"And?"

"And I'm glad I'm not blind, so I don't hit this damn coffee table every time I chase you around it."

"And?"

"And I'm glad I can tell you I love you, which I should have said two months ago."

Her heart filled. "Has it been that long?"

"At least."

Their kiss was long, deep and ended in a kind of space and contentment Cliff had never guessed would be his. But there was a question nagging him, too.

"Total honesty, right?" He paused, marshaling his courage, watching her solemnly nod. "I can't move the Imperial Mine."

She gave him a look that said, "That couldn't be it, could it?" His big question? "My business is fairly portable," she told him. "Maybe not the therapy part, but if you don't mind my saying so, on a shared income I might get by with pottery alone."

"Sounds well reasoned to me. I enjoyed this last fair." He'd more than enjoyed it. He'd used a break in the action to seek out a jeweler Annie had mentioned. Hammered gold and silver, rings in particular, matching but individual, handcrafted by someone who cared. He hoped Annie liked his selection. It was burning a hole in his pocket even now. Could it matter if they waited until he was cleared to return to work?

Annie was right, though. There were times when the past intruded on the present. "Linda had this thing about living that far north."

"She missed out, didn't she?"

He smiled a dashing smile of thanks that made Annie quiver like a violin string. "That's what I always thought."

He kissed her again, then leaned back. He couldn't get enough of looking at her. Her hair was full of firelight, reddish-brown, highlights like dancing flame. "I love your hair like this, by firelight. On my pillow, in my hands. Heck," he growled, "I love *you* on my pillow and in my hands."

Tumbling back on the sofa, he found her hands resting exactly where he wanted them, where his desire grew under the soft weight of her palm. "You're getting daring."

"Mmm."

"You know what I'd like? You on a blanket of leaves."

"Want to get me outside again, eh?"

"Just think of the fall colors, the reds and golds and you, pale and pink."

"And Kane, chasing deer and barking his head off."

"And retrieving our clothes every time we drop them."

"Speaking of which."

"He's whining to be let out."

"Mmm-hmm." Annie smiled.

Cliff sighed. "Is it my turn?"

"It's your dog."

Alone for a moment, she sat in front of fireplace savoring the wine and the love. She turned the glass around in her hands, thinking about the sparks given off by wine, firelight and dark brown eyes.

He said he loved her.

She believed every word of it. "Back so soon?"

"He's staying out on his chain tonight. He can sleep in his doghouse or bay at the moon."

"Animal lover."

"This particular animal. Care to claw my back, little cat?"

She did a so-so imitation of a cat's purr, but it was the lowered eyelids and come-hither look that undid him. She was right—talking helped. Cliff felt closer to her, relieved of secrets of his own making. He loved her. And while they made exquisite love in front of the fireplace, and later in a body-warmed bed, he told her so again and again.

In the middle of the night, Cliff woke up. Wine headache, he thought. He didn't usually get them, but it had been quite a while since he'd had any wine. Annie was sated and sleeping and curled beside him in the dark. He could feel her there, just as he'd dreamed long before he'd ever actually had her there.

Not wanting to wake her, he carefully got out of bed and tucked the quilt around her. His teeth felt furry. If he was going to wake her with the kind of kiss he planned, brushing wouldn't be a bad idea.

He was naked. The house was cold. Reminding himself it was October and probably time to fire up the furnace, he shuffled through the discarded clothes at the foot of the bed. That was when he remembered the rings in the back pocket of his jeans. Touching them once for good luck, he hid them in the dresser drawer. In a matter of days he'd be back for them. Proposing, a once terrifying prospect, seemed so easy. She'd practically said yes last night.

He retraced his path to the bathroom. Used to do this all the time, he thought, full speed ahead. Used to have bruises up and down his shins, too. He stepped over another pile of clothes—Annie's.

Lowering himself gingerly onto the edge of the bed, he picked up what felt like silk—her blouse. Without sight he'd had sound. He rubbed the silk between his fingers and listened. Touch, that was there in his fingers, too, the fabric smooth and cool, not as warm as when he'd removed it from her. Smell, he raised it to his cheek, feeling the need for a shave as it caught and slid against stubble. He sniffed it. Yes. That delicate smell women have, the particular perfume Annie made, her body so sweet and loving last night.

Could a hundred "I love yous" convey what she meant to him right now? He wanted to wake her and tell her. He got up instead.

She was still lying on her side, facing the bathroom. He closed the door carefully before turning on the light.

With a burst of profanity, he slammed a hand over his eyes. Damn, why hadn't he brought his glasses in here! That white light was blinding.

He squinted, his eyes instantly sore, and fumbled for the toothpaste. At least he knew this routine with his eyes closed. Turning on the water, he opened his eyes just enough to smear on a rapid line of paste. As he brushed, he glanced up once out of sheer habit.

One look was all he needed.

His eyes were red. Blood red where the white should be. He stood and stared, the light cutting through him like a knife. He didn't care. The pain he'd mistaken for a headache was nothing compared to the panic.

"RSVP. Redness, Soreness, Vision, Photophobia." Three out of four symptoms. He was losing it. The transplant was being rejected. He was going blind again.

It couldn't have been that wine. Not half a glass!

It was a transplant, damn it. Anything could go wrong.

But could it be made right?

He dropped the toothpaste tube into the wastebasket with a thunk; he'd squeezed it flat. He sat numbly on the edge of the tub.

How long will I have to wait this time?

What if it fails again?

Half an hour was gone when he opened the bathroom door, letting a shaft of light fall across Annie. His heart lurched. She was beautiful, incredibly loving, and he'd found her when he'd been blind. "How lucky could a man get?" he thought, overcome with fury at the irony of it.

Why, God? Why now, when he was so close?

To think he'd almost asked her to marry him last night. He almost laughed, then didn't, for fear it would come out a sob. What he wanted, more than anything right now, was a convenient brick wall to ram his fist through.

He couldn't keep her. That's all there was to it. Not if he was getting back on that merry-go-round of waiting and hoping and relying on doctors. Not if there was any chance he could be permanently blind. He might have to face that prospect. There was no way in hell he'd ask it of her. Trouble was something you kept from other people. This was his problem alone.

He had to call the hospital in Ann Arbor, he thought, suddenly calm. He'd find out what he had to do, and whether he could drive there himself before it got worse.

But first, Annie would have to leave.

He took a deep breath, then another. Neither calmed his racing heart or the sick dread he felt. Let me look a little longer, he thought, memorizing her before he said goodbye.

Her eyelids fluttered.

His hand fumbled for the light switch and turned it off just in time.

"What time is it," she said drowsily.

Her voice was hoarse in the morning. No wonder he loved making love to her then. He'd like to right now.

"Don't get up," he said, striding to his side of the bed to grab his sunglasses off the side table. Pulling on a pair of jogging shorts and a sweatshirt, he laced his shoes, his back to her. "I'm taking Kane for a run."

"It's barely dawn."

He stopped in the doorway and came back, giving her a soft kiss on the forehead. "Go back to sleep."

Stay in my bed. Don't leave me.

He unwound her arms from around his neck and left.

Annie showered, humming to herself, laughing sometimes. She felt giggly and giddy and more than a little all right. She smoothed soap over her stomach, thinking how Cliff's lips had pressed there the night before. He loved her. He'd said so, many times.

She was still smiling when she shut off the blow dryer and heard him downstairs making breakfast.

Coming up behind him at the stove, she gave him a squeeze. He was still wearing his jogging suit, a line down his back dark with sweat. "You should change. You'll get a chill."

He didn't answer, cracking two more eggs into the pan.

Annie set the table. "Eyes bothering you today? You don't usually wear your sunglasses to breakfast."

"I do sometimes."

"Why not the adjusting lenses? It isn't that bright in here."

His fist clenched on the skillet handle, but he kept his face immobile. "Annie," he said with great patience, "you know how much I liked being hovered over."

That hurt. He didn't have to see her to know it. It was the way she stopped in midmotion, setting the orange juice so carefully down.

"Want your eggs over easy?" he ground out. What sense was there in keeping up the civilized pretense when he was about to do one of the lowest things he'd ever done?

"Over easy's fine." She ran her hands up and down her arms. "Chilly in here."

He clenched his jaw. If that was bait, he wasn't biting. His gut was in knots. He knew right now he wouldn't taste this food.

Sitting down at the table, he forced himself to eat. It was harder keeping his eyes away from her when all he wanted to do was look.

The toast popped. She was up before he was. "Jam?"

"No. I have to leave."

She stopped moving altogether, staring at the red raspberry jam smeared on the bread, knowing that in a few minutes it wouldn't matter whether he liked her friend's homemade jam better than any store-bought. She remembered the fair where they'd bought it, the sunshine, the laughter.

She'd remember this moment, too.

"I have to go to the Upper Peninsula," he said without emotion. "Check in with the mine doctor."

"What time will you be back?"

He didn't answer right away. This he didn't want to see. "I don't know if I'll be coming back."

He looked anyway; he couldn't help it. From behind the sunglasses he wondered why God let him see again if this was all he'd have to remember Annie by—the hurt and anguish, her determination not to let it show, the courage it took her not to crumble, not in front of him.

All right, look, you selfish bastard, look what you're doing to her. All because you couldn't wait.

Annie swallowed a bite of toast, thinking it would never go down. When he'd left so abruptly this morning, she'd been afraid but only for a moment. He'd kissed her before going and the fear had vanished. How easily she could be fooled by a gesture, one of his gestures.

When she decided her hands weren't shaking all that badly, she took a sip of her juice. "That's it then," she said, swallowing mechanically.

"I'm sorry." They were the only words that would come out, the only words that weren't "I love you." He felt like choking on them.

Eleven

Annie couldn't remember how she got home, only that she was here, hugging herself on the couch, feeling like a scarecrow with the stuffing pulled out.

She'd half expected this. But never, never had she imagined it would end so abruptly. How? Why? He'd said he loved her. He'd meant it. Unless she'd been wrong about him all along.

Over the next few days she went through the motions. She couldn't work on her pottery, something about touching, creating; there were too many memories of Cliff out there in the studio.

One morning she woke up. Here she was hiding from the only other thing she loved in life, the thing that might get her through this if she worked hard enough, concentrated hard enough. Marching into her studio like an army retaking a hill, she purposely sought out the pots Cliff had made. Hurled against the wall, the first broke with a satisfying smash. She reached for the chimes. They sang when she touched them, a plaintive ache, and she couldn't destroy them. That was when she sat down and cried.

How could he? Why? Was she that easily fooled?

And what about him? Was the Cliff Sullivan she'd known through so much pain capable of this coldness? Leading a woman on then dropping her the moment he was healed? She reached over to pick up the broken vase. Like an unsolvable puzzle, the pieces just didn't fit.

"No, Mr. Sullivan, you are not going to discard me like this. I will not go gentle into that good night. In that way we are a lot alike. I'm going to do some raging of my own."

She'd gone it alone, carrying her pain inside, not wanting to burden anyone else with her problems. Wasn't that his way of dealing with things? Well, she'd show him. Real strength meant being vulnerable, reaching out. She'd reach out one more time and demand an explanation. Not yelling, not crying, simply asking and deserving an answer. She loved that man, period. He'd said he loved her.

Annie marched down the beach and pounded on the cottage door. No answer. She went around to the window. It was easy to see inside. The setting sun lit up the inside of the cottage like a movie set. There was no one there. Walking slowly around to the road, feeling the revitalizing determination that accompanied her down the beach seeping away, she noticed the bowls in Kane's pen were empty and dry, his chain hung up. Whatever tire tracks Cliff's car had left were blown over with sand. He was gone, had been for days.

He'd returned to the Upper Peninsula, two hundred miles and a world away. It was over.

* * *

Annie didn't know what day it was, how many it had been. Autumn so far was cold and damp, cloudy and miserable, but the weather had nothing on her mood. She worked because she had to, taught because she had to. She signed up to teach Pottery I, Evening Session, at the local college. And never stopped thinking about Cliff.

That was why it didn't really surprise her two weeks after the breakup to glance up one day and see a man who looked like him walking slowly down the beach, head bowed to the wind. At first she thought she was imagining it, the sunglasses on a stormy gray day, the shoulders hunched. He kept walking, hugging close to the water's edge. She kept looking.

The next time. Two days later. After dawn. The garage door was down, but Annie had used every excuse to get up and glance out, finishing pot after pot, filling up shelves. This time there was no doubt. He had Kane with him, in the harness.

It was a public beach, she reasoned. The man could go where he wanted.

Like hell.

Holding her hand-loomed sweater closed against the October wind, Annie stalked across the sand toward him. "Why are you haunting me?" Let him deny it. Let him say he was just walking the dog. She wanted explanations.

After a long expressionless look, all he said was "I wanted to see you." His jaw was tight and clenched, sprinkled with the beginnings of another beard. He turned his head to the pounding water.

The question tore out of her. "Why?"

He tugged Kane into a sitting position. "I had to leave."

"You could have told me if you needed time. I wasn't pressuring you." And she'd be damned if she'd apologize, either.

"It wasn't your fault. It was mine. I had to be certain about my eyes."

"So we waited."

"We went too far. The first time I made love to you I was past the point of going back. I loved you too much."

Past tense.

Annie swallowed the metallic taste of brittle wind and damned-up tears. Confusion reigned over every other emotion warring within her. Nothing he said made sense; she needed so many reasons and none of the ones he gave fit.

"Annie." He touched her arm the way he used to, when he wanted to know exactly where she was. "I'm sorry I came back. I should have stayed away."

Without another word, not a goodbye, he turned and walked down the beach. Annie didn't chase him, didn't call. He didn't look back.

He couldn't.

It took every ounce of Cliff's shredded patience not to slam the phone into its cradle. He hated asking for help in the first place, and his little brother wasn't making it any easier. "Dave, for the last time—"

"I can't. I told you. It's not a matter of wanting to. The transmission is shot. It's in pieces on the garage floor."

"Why did you take it apart when you knew I needed a ride?"

"Because I can't drive with a busted transmission!"

"Then borrow a car."

"It's the Saturday of the Ohio State game. Everybody's out of town."

"So rent a car!"

"You know you wouldn't cosign a credit card for me. Can't rent a car without one. Or leave home," he muttered.

"This is my operation, damn it! I can't snap my fingers and get another transplant whenever—"

"Don't you think I know that?"

The shouting stopped. Tension and silence hung in the air as Dave thought back over the past two weeks. He'd made four trips up north to bring Cliff down for the steroid treatments that were meant to halt the rejection. They'd slowed it, but it hadn't stopped. And yet after each visit, Cliff insisted on going back to the cottage. Why, Dave wondered, if he was so intent on calling things off with Annie?

The whole situation ticked him off. Was his brother totally blind? You didn't find a woman like that and let her get away. Maybe it was time he lectured Cliff for a change.

Then an idea dawned. Maybe a busted transmission wasn't such a bad deal. "Can't you get a ride from someone up there?"

They both knew who he was referring to. Even picturing going to her for help made Cliff wince. It would mean dragging her into his problems. He'd designed this self-made hell specifically to avoid that. He clenched the receiver in his fist. "You're the only one I've got."

Pride was one thing, Dave reasoned, but Cliff wasn't crazy enough to risk his sight for it. He leaned back on the couch and counted to ten. These day rates must be really adding up. "Sorry, bro, there's just nothing I can do about that transmission. You couldn't get a bus ticket or something?''

On Cliff's end the receiver slammed down.

''Ooh-eee!'' Dave whistled. That was one angry, bullheaded man.

Cliff tipped his head back for more eye drops. At the very least they might delay the rejection enough to prevent permanent damage to his eyes. The transplant was scheduled for Monday. He'd been watching his vision blur a little more each day. At least the accident had been immediate, a ripping explosion of sand and particles. This time there was an unreal nightmare quality to it, like slipping down a dark hole in slow motion, unable to claw your way to the light or call out to the only one who could save you, for fear she'd be pulled down, too.

Kane panted eagerly by the back door as Cliff headed into the kitchen. Stopping at the fridge to grab a soda, he remembered Annie this morning on the beach. He hadn't mentioned it to Dave. Furiously he slammed his palm against the counter. How could his brother be so cavalier? He *needed* that operation. He had to get back to Annie as soon as possible. It might already be too late.

This morning she'd looked angry, hurt and confused. Was that all he'd ever see in her eyes? Better than pity, he thought disgustedly. Or the hurt and worry he was sparing her by keeping this to himself. He was determined not to drag her through it, had been ever since he'd admitted to himself how much he loved her.

So why was he reaching for Kane's harness one more time? Why was it so imperative he see Annie once more?

Because he had to.

Because he loved her.

Because bitter, furious or indifferent, hers was the only face he wanted to see—even if it was the last thing he ever saw.

Especially if it was the last.

The sunset was a lustrous red slashed with orange. A shape was coming down the beach toward him. Cliff braced himself. He didn't want to argue with her, just look at her.

Annie wasn't about to argue. She had her explanation. Far from leaving her at peace, it left her feeling as roiled as the waves. "Dave called."

"He what?" Cliff replied sharply.

"He says you need a ride to Ann Arbor and he can't give you one. He asked me."

Cliff said nothing, that unreadable look of his firmly in place. She wanted to snatch those damn glasses off his nose. "You didn't want me to know, did you?"

"I had to make you leave. If this operation fails, I'd have nothing to offer you."

"You should have told me."

"So you'd stick around? Pity me?"

"When have I *ever* done that? You made up your mind what I could take and what was too much to ask, but did you ever ask me?" She clutched her sweater to her and whipped the hair out of her face, waiting until she could trust herself to keep the anguish out of her voice. He was in pain, emotional pain, real pain, and God, he was so alone. "Cliff, please."

She tried to touch his cheek. He drew back as if stung. "Look at this, Annie. This is exactly what I wanted to avoid. It's hurting you just knowing. I didn't want you hurt."

"So you were going to keep it to yourself."

"Yes."

"Has it ever occurred to you how selfish that is? You freeze me out every time you insist on being alone."

Alone? Hardly. She'd always been inside him, able to walk right into his heart. Through his sense of smell, his hearing, his skin, she got in, perfume and jangling bracelets and frizzy hair. He'd never been able to bar the door against her—only by leaving—and then he hadn't been able to stay away.

"You only let me share the good times," she said. "When it came to the most important event in your life, I wasn't allowed to even care."

"Maybe I wasn't as much afraid of hurting you as of losing you."

"How?" she cried. "I love you. I loved you when you were blind, when there were no guarantees—"

"But I believed that guarantee, that I'd get well. I had to. This time I'm not so sure."

"Do you think I'd stop loving you?"

He took so long to answer that she thought he hadn't heard. Then he spoke, more to the waves than to her. "I'm afraid I'd drive you away. I can be grumpy as a bear—"

She hastily wiped tears off her cheeks. "I've lived through grumpy."

"And frustrated and insecure and I'm not above being mean. I don't want to put you through that, either, not again. I don't think I could stand to see that happen twice."

"I told you once that love was unconditional. That means you can be imperfect, too."

She could tell by the way he leveled his gaze at her that he could still see something. The frown said it all. "Like

I was the other morning? Treating you the way I did? Is that forgivable, Annie?''

She could almost count the heartbeats. He was giving her a way in. Anything was forgivable. She named her terms. "The only thing I can't deal with is you shutting me out. If I had to wonder about every mood, every time, wondering if you were hiding something or if something else had gone wrong, I couldn't stand that. Love is sharing. It has to be. Communicating. Maybe you've lived too long alone, keeping your problems to yourself.''

She kicked the sand. It flew back at her, stinging her legs. He hunched inside his jacket and turned to go.

"You almost asked me to marry you," she said to the wind. "In health but not in sickness, was that it?''

He didn't answer.

She didn't expect him to. "It's ironic. I was afraid you wouldn't love me if I didn't measure up. Instead, you won't love me because you're not good enough.''

She was baiting him, and he knew it. He stopped walking.

"Let me call in," she said. "Tell them I won't be in Monday. Then I'll give you that ride to Ann Arbor.''

"Annie.''

Half of her didn't want to hear it, whatever he was going to say. In a way it was easier to call it quits, wrap herself up in her memories and never get hurt again. "Hurry up. It's cold out here.''

He tried to decipher exactly how angry she was. He missed that keen hearing he'd had. But as long as there was a shred of fading light, he'd look. "I had to see you. I couldn't stay away.''

"Then don't push me away! Let me be part of your life. That's all there is to it." She wanted to yell, throw another pot. How could she get through to him?

"I don't want to tie you down."

Letting out an angry sigh, she laughed. "Sounds kinky, but I'm game if you are."

His voice was harsh, choked. "That isn't what I meant and you know it."

"*Ask me then*. Don't decide for me!" She trudged up the beach, trusting him to follow. She was so furious that she wanted to shake him. At the top of the last dune before her house, she turned on him. "Listen to me, Cliff Sullivan. I love who I please. It's *my* choice, and for that reason alone I'll never be tied down. Understand?"

He nodded. She was in front of the most glorious sunset he'd ever seen. Reds, slashes of purple, bands of turquoise and the deep blues of night creeping in overhead. None of them were as beautiful as she.

It was a nasty trick of fate, her coming along at exactly the wrong time, insisting on helping him, on being part of his struggle, when all he wanted was to be alone. No matter what the future brought, he had a feeling he'd thank that trick of fate for the rest of his life. And thank that honesty of hers; that might be the biggest lesson she'd ever taught him. "You don't care how grumpy I get?"

"Of course I do. It's a pain in the butt."

He fought a grin, tugging Kane along as he stepped closer. "In sickness and in health?"

"That's how it goes."

He handed over Kane's harness, and Annie took it with a surprised look. Not as surprised as when he produced the ring from his back pocket. "Turn toward the light. If it's the last thing I see, I want to see this."

His fingers were a little stiff, the temperature having dropped as the sun set behind the horizon. But when the ring was on her finger, Annie clenched her fist as if daring it to ever get away. "You haven't been carrying that around all this time?" It was a dumb question, but she knew anything else might result in a sob of sheer joy.

"I grabbed it before I left the house. I figured if I was going to get down on my knees and beg you to take me back, I'd better be prepared."

A picture of Cliff getting down on his knees for anything was downright unimaginable. Annie's doubtful expression said as much.

"If I came here one more time, I would have been. You're marrying a desperate man." He kissed her, quickly catching the tear that spilled onto her cheek. His lips were far from satisfied with a little salty water. They wanted the true taste of her, musky and womanly, lips and tongues and places that opened only for him.

Annie rasped her cheek against his, loving the familiar scratch of the new beard. When it was long, she'd love it even more. And when he shaved it off, and when she asked him to grow it back, and...

He pressed his lips to her ear, inhaling the sweet smell of perfume that lingered in her hair. "Want me to get down on one knee and ask you to be Mrs. Annie Sullivan?"

"Oh, no!" she gasped, tearing her mouth away from his. "I couldn't do that."

"Why not?" For a second doubts flickered across his brow.

"Annie Sullivan was Helen Keller's teacher! I'm no miracle worker."

"To me you are."

"This Rosetti is going to stay a Rosetti. Okay with you?"

She wiped the hair back from his forehead, took off his sunglasses and looked into his eyes. They looked sore, tired, worried, but they looked at her with unmistakable love.

"About the operation," he began.

"All doubts and fears you share with me," she stated unequivocally. "I love you now. I've *already* loved you through good and bad, grumpy and happy, sleepy and dopey and all the other seven dwarfs."

He tried very hard to reverse his smile to a frown. "Do I have to do all the worrying in this family myself?"

"Definitely not," she insisted. She shook her head and pursed her lips, realizing she could skim them over his that way very easily. Pleasantly, too. "But for now, stop worrying and tell me you love me."

"I love you. Now what about the future?"

She quieted him with another kiss and a smile. "Want to rent a hotel room in Ann Arbor? If we go down tonight, we could practice making love in the dark."

"This is your idea of worrying?"

"No, this is my idea of sharing. You can share the good things, too, you know."

"Teach me."

"I will, Cliff," she breathed. "I will."

"And forgive me?"

"Yes."

"And love me?"

"Always."

Epilogue

Walking through the crowded art fair, Cliff knew people were looking at him. The guide-dog harness on Kane made them clear a path, eyes averted more often than not. Sometimes he heard them pointing Kane out to their children. Or the women commenting on Alice, walking like the rambunctious two-year-old she was, one chubby leg in front of the other, clinging to Cliff's other hand.

Funny how he didn't really mind what people thought anymore. Let 'em think what they want, as Annie always said.

He heard the chimes from her booth tinkling up ahead. They'd set up on the first left-hand turn. The sounds made it easy to find. Even Kane noticed, tugging harder, Alice bubbling along in her made-up language.

Annie glanced up, her smile spreading wide, her heart turning over at the sight of them. It always affected her that way. Her bearded, blond husband in those mysterious and sexy shades, striding ahead as confident as ever, their towheaded toddler in tow. Alice was the only thing that could make Cliff shorten his stride. And then there was Kane, the sturdy black tugboat bringing them safely back to her.

As Alice made a detour for the carved wooden toys, Annie took the opportunity to simply watch. Cliff's hair was shorter now, neat, above his ears. Thanks to the beard, she didn't miss that wild Samson she'd met on the beach so long ago. It seemed like a million years, or a handful of days. Either way she had a heartful of memories, the greatest of which was their daughter.

The corner of Annie's mouth turned up in a smile as she attempted to listen to a customer.

He could still turn women's heads, she couldn't help noticing. And she could work up a bout of jealousy at the drop of a hat. Not that it was necessary. He seemed to love her more as time went by, not less.

"We're back," he said.

"No!" Alice said.

Annie bid farewell to the customer and sank back into her director's chair. The child needed attention first. "Want to climb in Mommie's lap?"

"No!"

"Her favorite word," Cliff murmured.

"You don't say."

"Don't you contradict me, too. I even got 'no' to an ice-cream cone."

"No!" Annie laughed. "Even that?"

"How would I have carried it back?" Cliff shrugged.

The motion made Annie picture the shoulders and chest covered by his knit shirt. She caught her breath. "You did look like you had your hands full."

He rested one hand on the back of her chair and leaned over to whisper in her ear. "I can think of a couple of things I'd rather fill my hands with."

Alice decided that now was the perfect time to clamber onto Annie's lap, tugging herself into a sitting position from which she could pat Kane's broad black head. "Kay," she said, sweetly offering her two-year-old's version of the Lab's name.

"Maybe later," Annie said softly, touching Cliff's hand. "I missed you while you were gone."

He bent to kiss her across the little girl's head. Alice reached up and pulled his sunglasses off.

Cliff squinted and stifled a curse.

"Don't, honey," Annie said, retrieving the glasses where Alice had tossed them onto the ground. "The light hurts your father's eyes." As she handed them back, she stroked his cheek with her hand. "And he has such beautiful eyes."

Cliff looked at her, long and silent. The love they shared had been spoken, nights in bed, mornings over coffee, evenings making love. In hospitals and a maternity ward, they'd shared their fears and hopes. But there were times, like now, when Annie smiled up at him with their daughter in her lap and love in her eyes, that a look could say it all.

*   *   *   *   *

Silhouette Desire

COMING NEXT MONTH

BLUE CHIP BRIDE
Audra Adams

The deal seemed simple: Janet Demarest married
Ken Radnor and in a year Ken would buy Janet's
stock in the Radnor Corporation, after which they'd
get their marriage annulled.
Simple … until Ken decided he wanted a great deal
more …

SEEING IS BELIEVING
Janet Bieber

He must be absolutely shameless! Lynda Fischer
was shocked to find herself attracted to the gorgeous
hunk that someone had hired to do a striptease on
her birthday. Little did she know that Kent
Berringer had been unscrupulously blackmailed by
his sister into delivering her birthday greetings. They
had been set up!

TAGGED
Lass Small

Four times a bridesmaid and not once the bride;
Fredricka Lambert's family were beginning to
despair of her. Then lifelong family friend Colin
Kilgallon decided that enough was enough; waiting
for Fredricka to notice him was taking far too long!

Silhouette Desire

COMING NEXT MONTH

SHILOH'S PROMISE
B J James

April's *Man of the Month*, Shiloh Butler, was a dark, brooding man. He'd sworn to protect his friend's widow, Megan Sullivan, from danger — but who would protect Megan from him?

INTERLUDE
Donna Carlisle

Wealthy, good-looking, intelligent — Alan Donovan was all that and more. But it didn't seem to amount to much when he was trapped in his car during a sudden blizzard … Luckily, capable, competent Colorado native Paula Mercer knew how to handle an emergency.

ULTERIOR MOTIVES
Laura Leone

Ross Tanner looked awfully good to Shelley Baird. He was suave, charming and debonair. But that was before she realized that he worked for the opposition!

Coming in April

TAGGED
by Lass Small

Fredricka Lambert had always believed in true love,
but she couldn't work out whom to love ... until
lifelong friend Colin Kilgallon pointed her in the
right direction — towards himself.

Fredricka is one of five fascinating Lambert sisters.
She is as enticing as each one of her four sisters,
whose stories you have already enjoyed.

- Hillary in GOLDILOCKS AND THE BEHR
  - Tate in HIDE AND SEEK
  - Georgina in RED ROVER
  - Roberta in ODD MAN OUT

Don't miss the last book of this enticing mini series,
only from Silhouette Desire.

Experience the thrill of

4
Silhouette
· Desires ·

absolutely free!

An irresistible offer from
• Silhouette •

Here's a personal invitation from Silhouette to become a regular reader of Desire; and to welcome you, we'd like you to have four books, an enchanting pair of glass oyster dishes and a special MYSTERY GIFT - absolutely free.

Then, each month you could look forward to receiving 6 more Desires delivered direct to your door, post and packing free. Plus our newsletter featuring author news, competitions and special offers.

This invitation comes with no strings attached. You can cancel or suspend your subscription at any time, and still keep your free books and gifts.

It's so easy. Send no money now. Simply fill in the coupon below at once and post to

Reader Service, FREEPOST, PO Box 236, Croydon, Surrey CR9 9EL.

FREE GIFT

A SURPRISE MYSTERY GIFT

POST TODAY!

- - - ✂ - - - - - - - - - - - - - - - - - - - no stamp required -

YES!

Please rush me my 4 Free Desires and 2 Free Gifts!

Please also reserve me a Reader Service Subscription - If I decide to subscribe I can look forward to receiving 6 Brand new Desires each month, for just £8.40. If I choose not to subscribe I shall write within 10 days - I can keep the books and gifts whatever I decide. I can cancel or suspend my subscription at any time. I am over 18.

EP81SD

NAME _____

ADDRESS _____

_____

_____

_____ POSTCODE _____

SIGNATURE _____

MAILING PREFERENCE SERVICE